the GARFIELD show

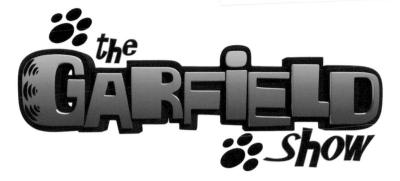

#7 "DESPERATELY SEEKING POOKY"

BASED ON THE ORIGINAL CHARACTERS CREATED BY

JIM DAVIS

PAPERCUTZ™
NEW YORK

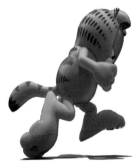

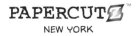

THE GARFIELD SHOW #7 "DESPERATELY SEEKING POOKY"
"THE GARFIELD SHOW" SERIES © 2017- DARGAUD MEDIA. ALL RIGHTS RESERVED. © PAWS. "GARFIELD" & GARFIELD CHARACTERS TM & ©️ PAWS
INC. - ALL RIGHTS RESERVED. THE GARFIELD SHOW-A DARGAUD MEDIA PRODUCTION. IN ASSOCIATION WITH FRANCE3 WITH THE PARTICIPATION
OF CENTRE NATIONAL DE LA CINÉMATOGRAPHIE AND THE SUPPORT OF REGION ILE-DE-FRANCE. BASED UPON THE CAHRACTERS CREATED BY
JIM DAVIS. ORIGINAL STORIES: "HIGH SCALE" WRITTEN BY PETER BERTS; "FREAKY MONDAY" WRITTEN BY JULIEN MAGNAT; "DESPERATELY
SEEKING POOKY" WRITTEN BY BAPTISTE HEIDRICH & JULIEN MONTHIEL.

TONY ISABELLA - SCRIPT RESTORATION AND ADDITIONAL DIALOGUE
TOM ORZECHOWSKI - LETTERING ON "HIGH SCALE" AND "FREAKY MONDAY"
WILSON RAMOS JR. - LETTERING ON "DESPERATELY SEEKING POOKY"
DAWN GUZZO - PRODUCTION COORDINATOR
ALEXANDER LU - EDITOR
JEFF WHITMAN - ASSISTANT MANAGING EDITOR
JIM SALICRUP
EDITOR-IN-CHIEF

ISBN: 978-1-62991-745-0

PRINTED IN KOREA
SEPTEMBER 2017

PAPERCUTZ BOOKS MAY BE PURCHASED FOR BUSINESS OR PROMOTIONAL USE. FOR INFORMATION ON BULK PURCHASES
PLEASE CONTACT MACMILLAN CORPORATE AND PREMIUM SALES DEPARTMENT AT (800) 221-7945 X5442.

DISTRIBUTED BY MACMILLAN
FIRST PAPERCUTZ PRINTING

GARFIELD

GRAPHIC NOVELS
AVAILABLE FROM
PAPERCUTZ™

THE GARFIELD SHOW #1
"UNFAIR WEATHER"

THE GARFIELD SHOW #2
"JON'S NIGHT OUT"

THE GARFIELD SHOW #3
"LONG LOST LYMAN"

THE GARFIELD SHOW #4
"LITTLE TROUBLE IN
BIG CHINA"

THE GARFIELD SHOW #5
"FIDO FOOD FELINE"

THE GARFIELD SHOW #6
"APPRENTICE SORCERER"

THE GARFIELD SHOW #7
"DESPERATELY SEEKING
POOKY"

THE GARFIELD SHOW GRAPHIC NOVELS ARE $7.99 IN PAPERBACK. VOLUMES 1-3 ARE $11.99 IN
HARDCOVER AND VOLUMES 4-6 ARE $12.99 HARDCOVER. VOLUME 7 IS $9.99, AVAILABLE IN
HARDCOVER ONLY. ALL VOLUMES ARE AVAILABLE FROM BOOKSELLERS EVERYWHERE.
YOU CAN ALSO ORDER ONLINE FROM WWW.PAPERCUTZ.COM. OR CALL 1-800-886-1223,
MONDAY THROUGH FRIDAY, 9-5 EST. MC, VISA, AND AMEX ACCEPTED. TO ORDER BY MAIL,
PLEASE ADD $5.00 FOR POSTAGE AND HANDLING FOR FIRST BOOK ORDERED, $1.00 FOR EACH
ADDITIONAL BOOK AND MAKE CHECK PAYABLE TO NBM PUBLISHING. SEND TO: PAPERCUTZ,
160 BROADWAY, SUITE 700, EAST WING, NEW YORK, NY 10038.

THE GARFIELD SHOW GRAPHIC NOVELS ARE ALSO AVAILABLE WHEREVER E-BOOKS ARE SOLD.

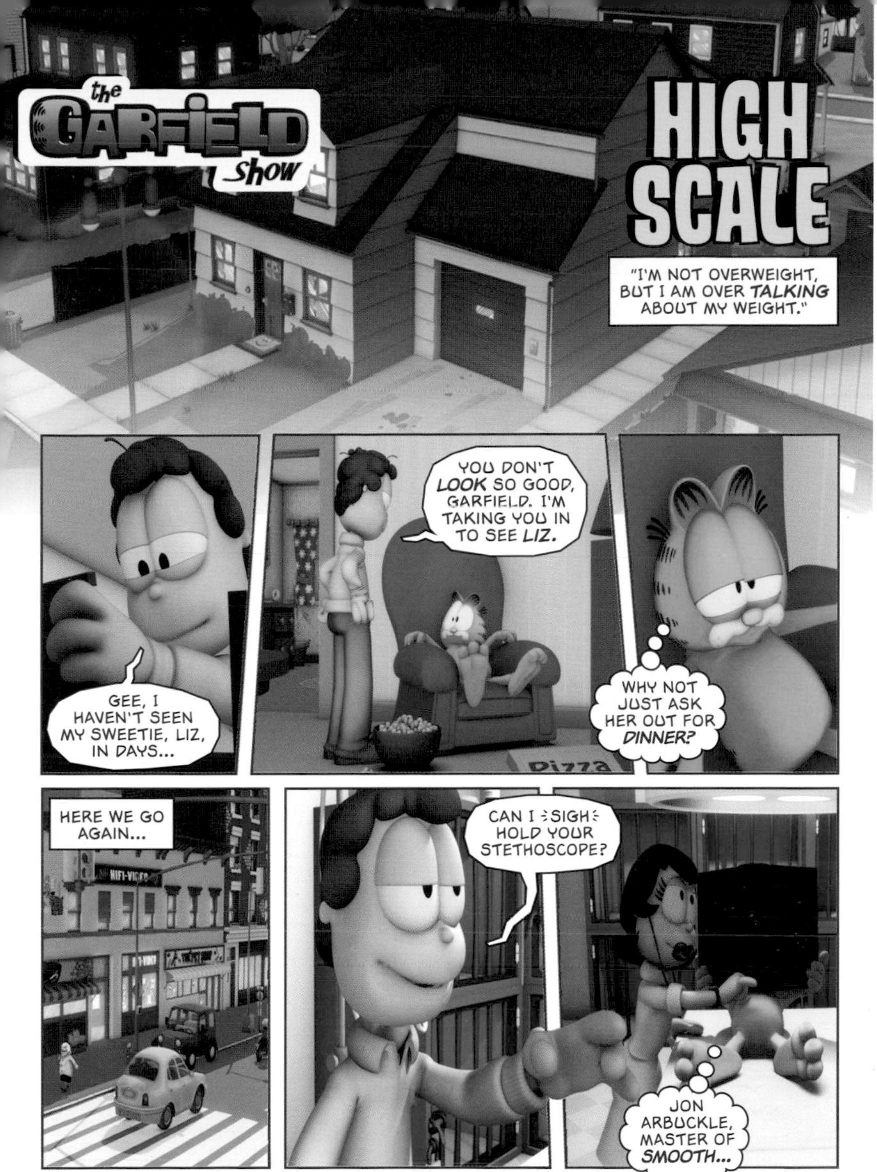
the GARFIELD show
HIGH SCALE
"I'M NOT OVERWEIGHT, BUT I AM OVER TALKING ABOUT MY WEIGHT."
GEE, I HAVEN'T SEEN MY SWEETIE, LIZ, IN DAYS...
YOU DON'T LOOK SO GOOD, GARFIELD. I'M TAKING YOU IN TO SEE LIZ.
PIZZA
WHY NOT JUST ASK HER OUT FOR DINNER?
HERE WE GO AGAIN...
HIFI-VIDEO
CAN I SIGH HOLD YOUR STETHOSCOPE?
JON ARBUCKLE, MASTER OF SMOOTH...

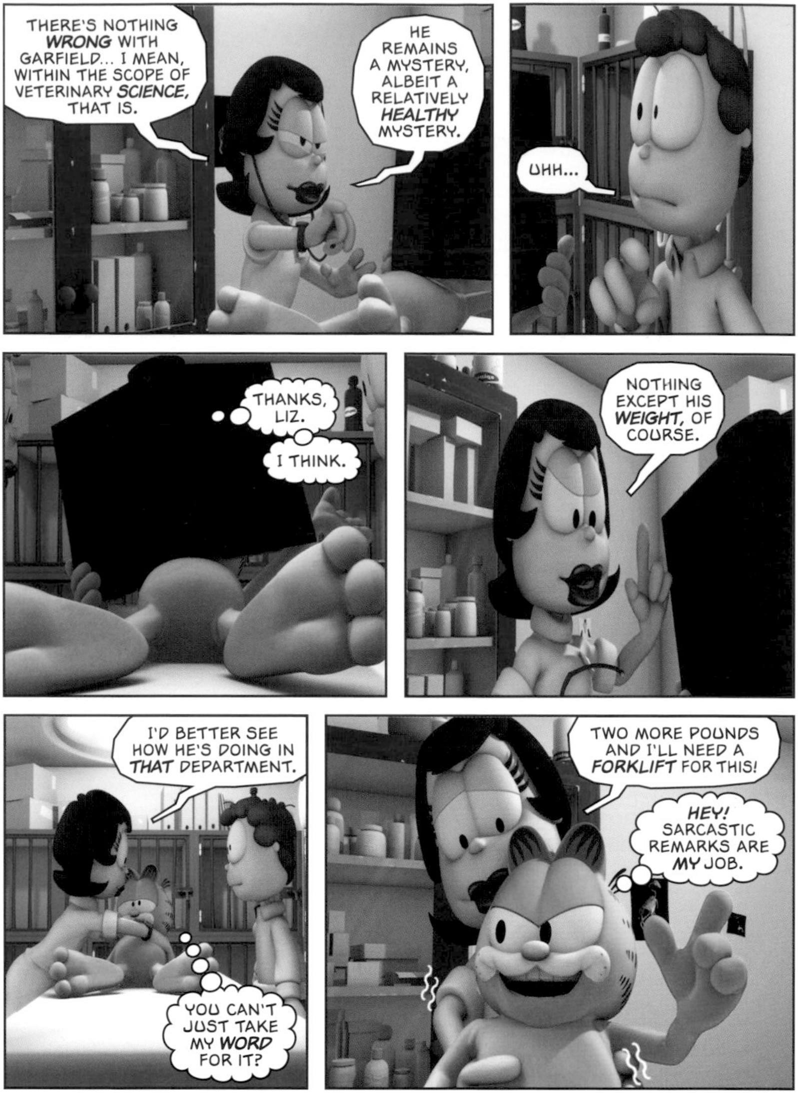
THERE'S NOTHING WRONG WITH GARFIELD... I MEAN, WITHIN THE SCOPE OF VETERINARY SCIENCE, THAT IS.
HE REMAINS A MYSTERY, ALBEIT A RELATIVELY HEALTHY MYSTERY.
UHH...
THANKS, LIZ.
I THINK.
NOTHING EXCEPT HIS WEIGHT, OF COURSE.
I'D BETTER SEE HOW HE'S DOING IN THAT DEPARTMENT.
YOU CAN'T JUST TAKE MY WORD FOR IT?
TWO MORE POUNDS AND I'LL NEED A FORKLIFT FOR THIS!
HEY! SARCASTIC REMARKS ARE MY JOB.

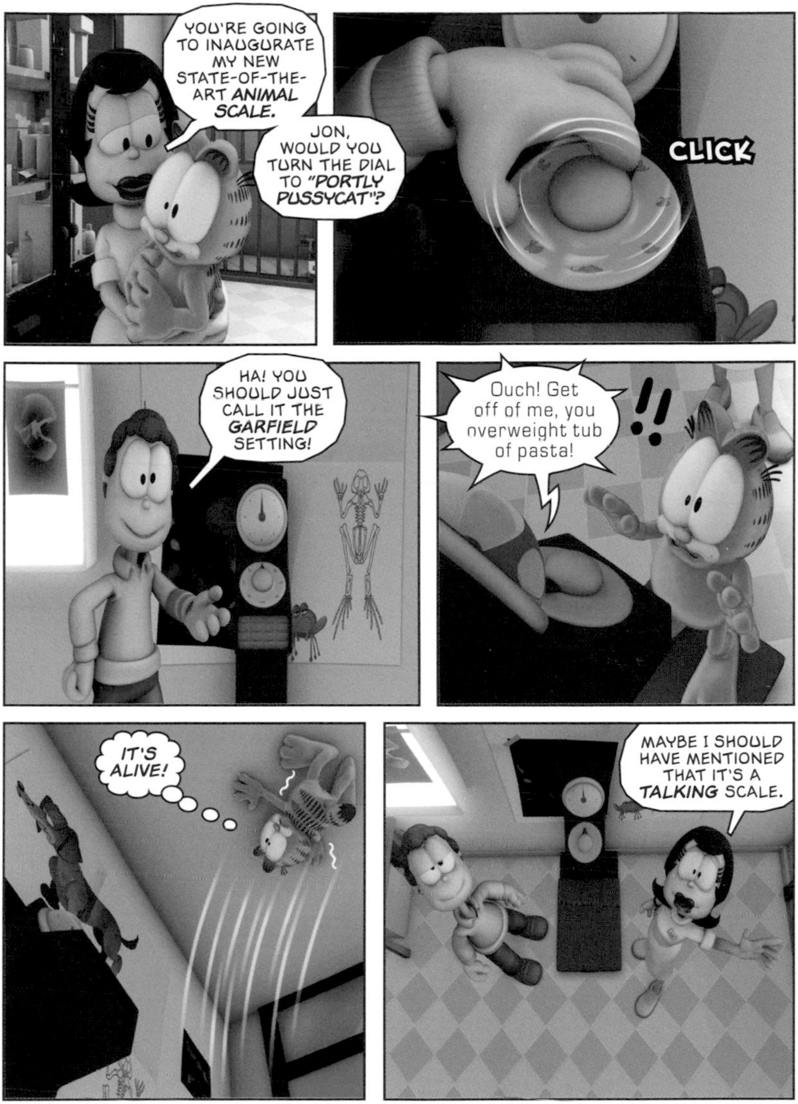
YOU'RE GOING TO INAUGURATE MY NEW STATE-OF-THE-ART ANIMAL SCALE.
JON, WOULD YOU TURN THE DIAL TO "PORTLY PUSSYCAT"?
CLICK
HA! YOU SHOULD JUST CALL IT THE GARFIELD SETTING!
Ouch! Get off of me, you overweight tub of pasta!
!!
IT'S ALIVE!
MAYBE I SHOULD HAVE MENTIONED THAT IT'S A TALKING SCALE.

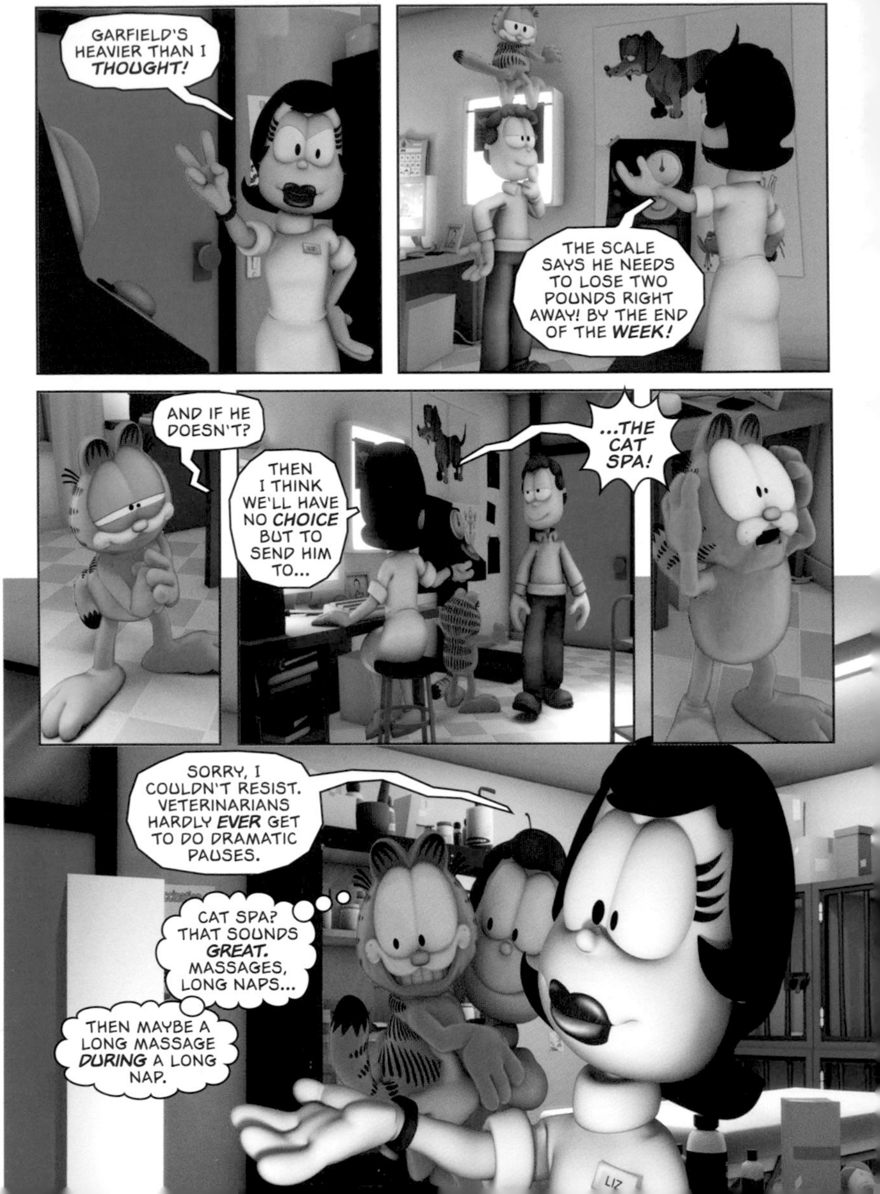
GARFIELD'S HEAVIER THAN I *THOUGHT!*
THE SCALE SAYS HE NEEDS TO LOSE TWO POUNDS RIGHT AWAY! BY THE END OF THE *WEEK!*
AND IF HE DOESN'T?
THEN I THINK WE'LL HAVE NO *CHOICE* BUT TO SEND HIM TO...
...THE CAT SPA!
SORRY, I COULDN'T RESIST. VETERINARIANS HARDLY *EVER* GET TO DO DRAMATIC PAUSES.
CAT SPA? THAT SOUNDS *GREAT.* MASSAGES, LONG NAPS...
THEN MAYBE A LONG MASSAGE *DURING* A LONG NAP.
LIZ

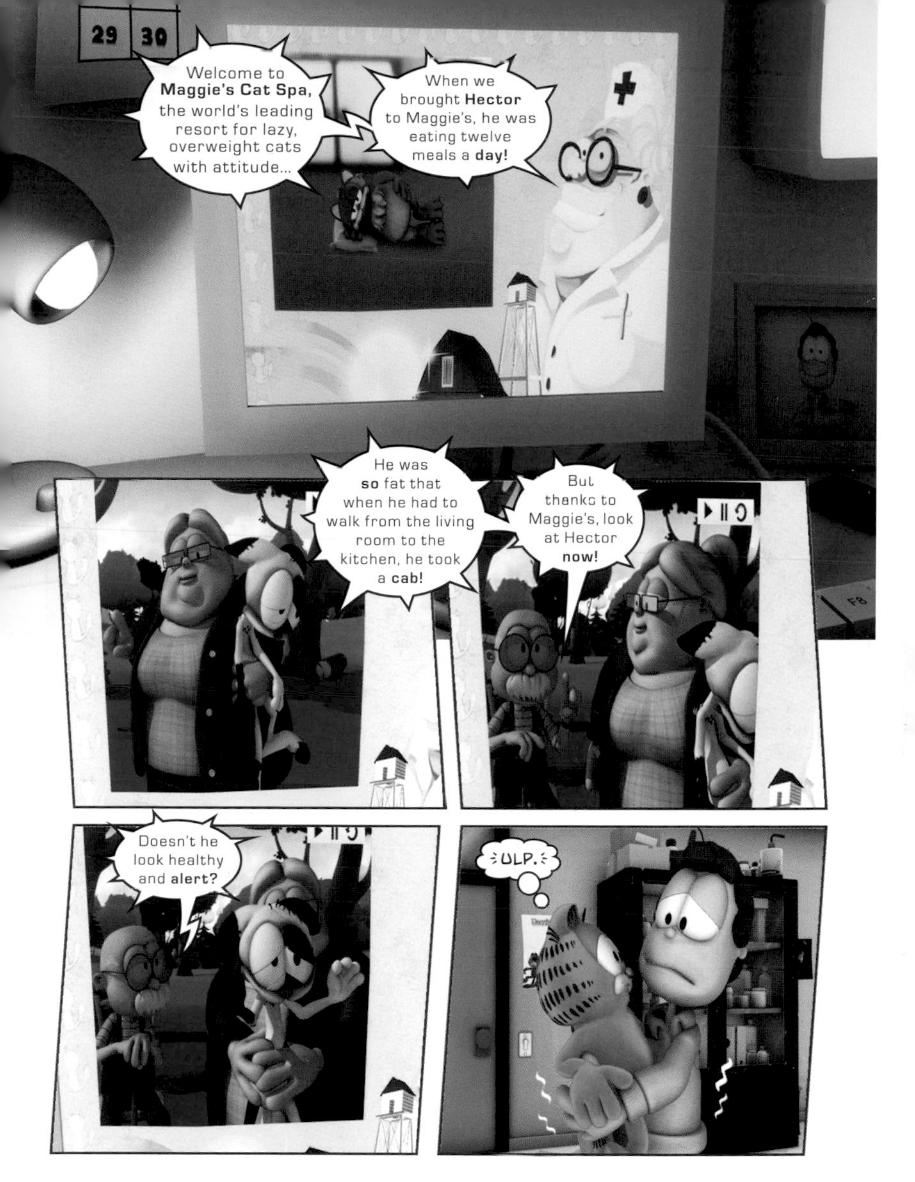
29 30
Welcome to Maggie's Cat Spa, the world's leading resort for lazy, overweight cats with attitude...
When we brought Hector to Maggie's, he was eating twelve meals a day!
He was so fat that when he had to walk from the living room to the kitchen, he took a cab!
But thanks to Maggie's, look at Hector now!
Doesn't he look healthy and alert?
ULP.

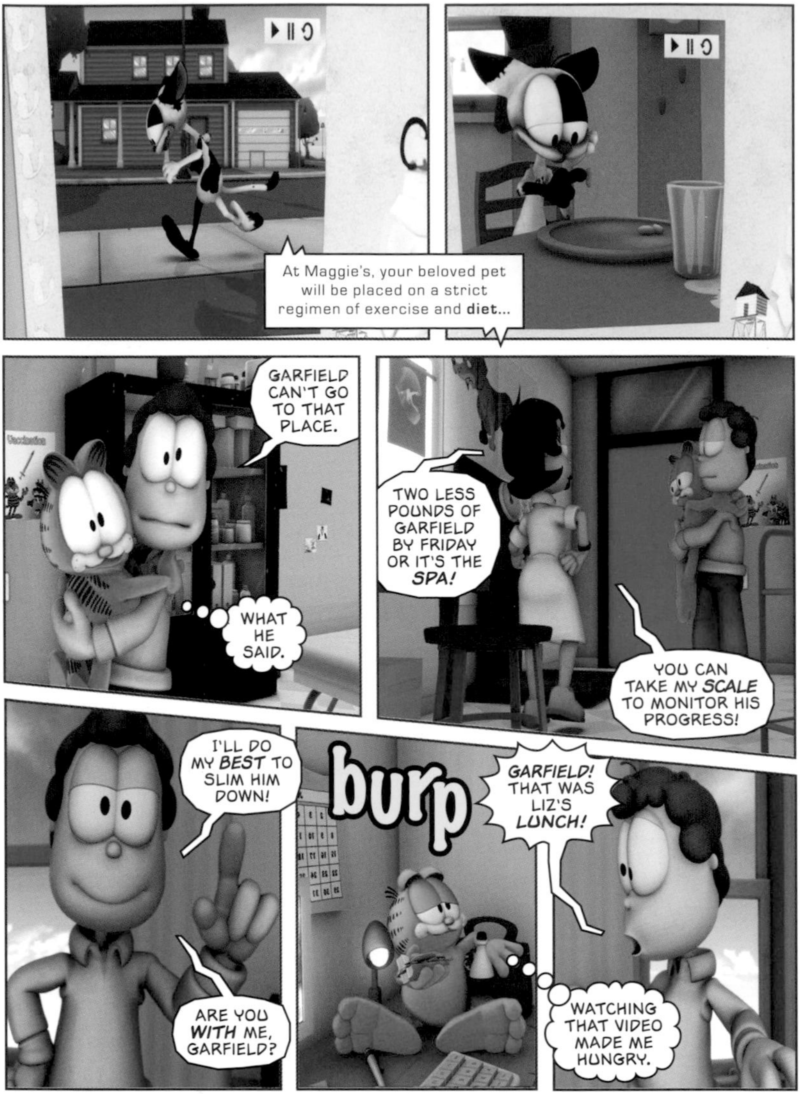
At Maggie's, your beloved pet will be placed on a strict regimen of exercise and **diet**...
GARFIELD CAN'T GO TO THAT PLACE.
WHAT HE SAID.
TWO LESS POUNDS OF GARFIELD BY FRIDAY OR IT'S THE *SPA!*
YOU CAN TAKE MY *SCALE* TO MONITOR HIS PROGRESS!
I'LL DO MY *BEST* TO SLIM HIM DOWN!
ARE YOU *WITH* ME, GARFIELD?
burp
GARFIELD! THAT WAS LIZ'S *LUNCH!*
WATCHING THAT VIDEO MADE ME HUNGRY.

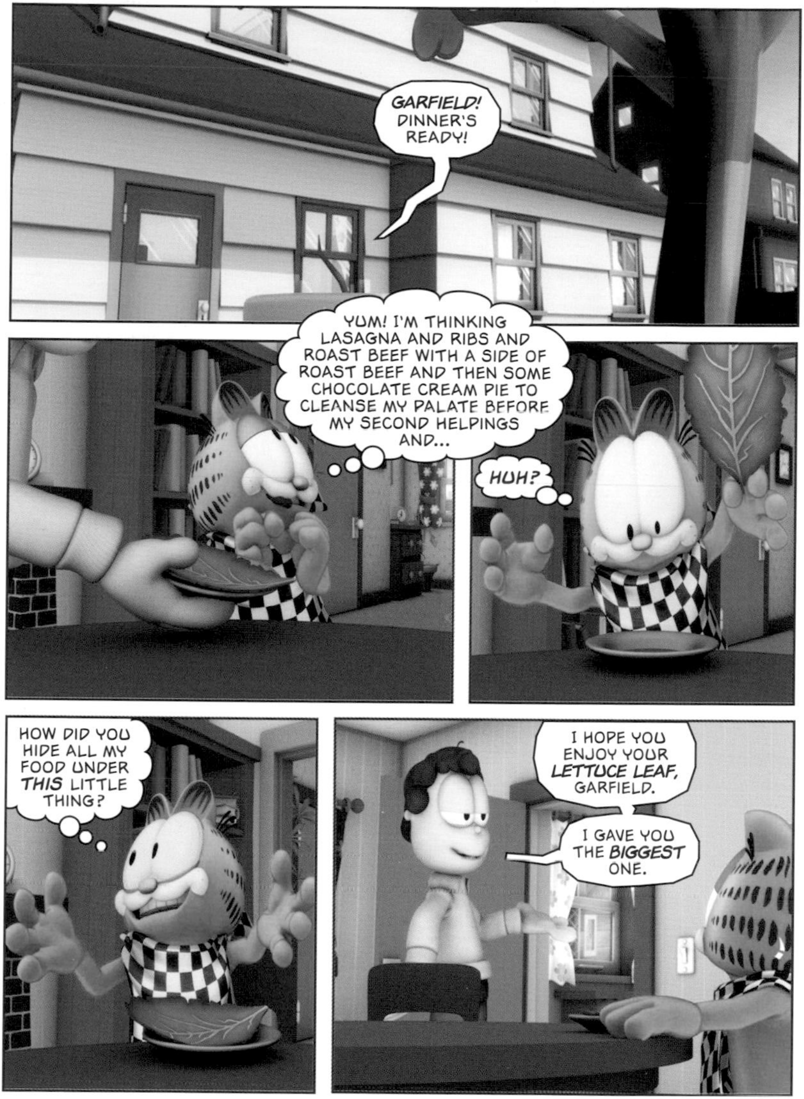
GARFIELD! DINNER'S READY!
YUM! I'M THINKING LASAGNA AND RIBS AND ROAST BEEF WITH A SIDE OF ROAST BEEF AND THEN SOME CHOCOLATE CREAM PIE TO CLEANSE MY PALATE BEFORE MY SECOND HELPINGS AND...
HUH?
HOW DID YOU HIDE ALL MY FOOD UNDER THIS LITTLE THING?
I HOPE YOU ENJOY YOUR LETTUCE LEAF, GARFIELD.
I GAVE YOU THE BIGGEST ONE.

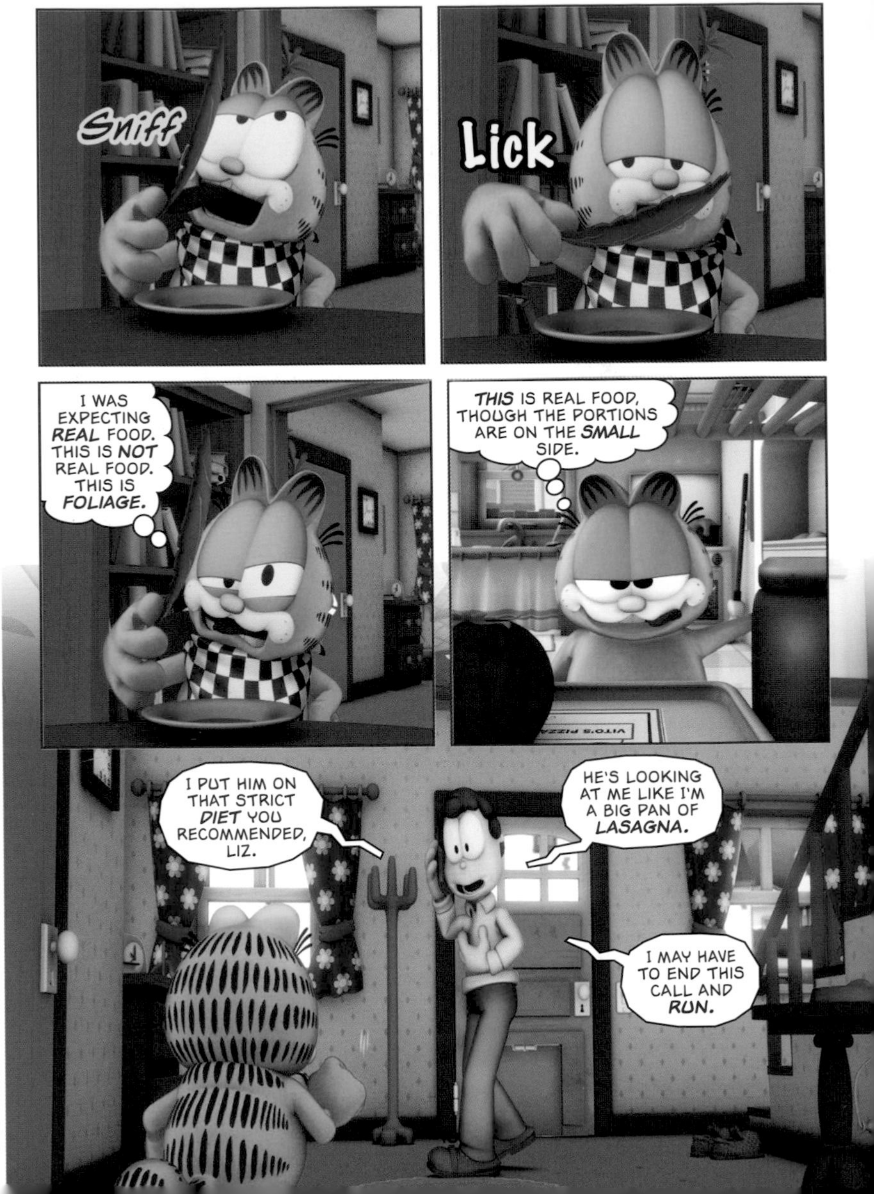

Sniff
Lick
I WAS EXPECTING REAL FOOD. THIS IS NOT REAL FOOD. THIS IS FOLIAGE.
THIS IS REAL FOOD, THOUGH THE PORTIONS ARE ON THE SMALL SIDE.
I PUT HIM ON THAT STRICT DIET YOU RECOMMENDED, LIZ.
HE'S LOOKING AT ME LIKE I'M A BIG PAN OF LASAGNA.
I MAY HAVE TO END THIS CALL AND RUN.

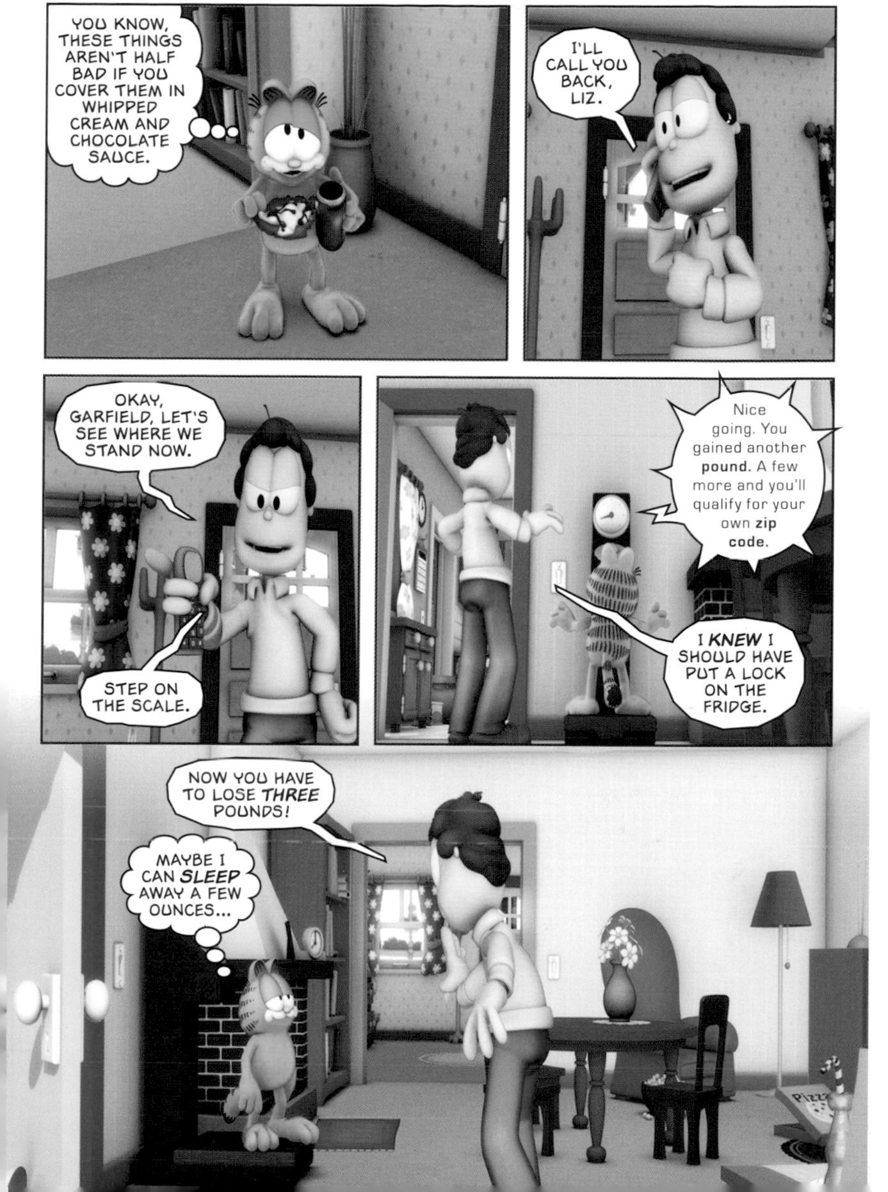

YOU KNOW, THESE THINGS AREN'T HALF BAD IF YOU COVER THEM IN WHIPPED CREAM AND CHOCOLATE SAUCE.
I'LL CALL YOU BACK, LIZ.
OKAY, GARFIELD, LET'S SEE WHERE WE STAND NOW.
STEP ON THE SCALE.
Nice going. You gained another **pound.** A few more and you'll qualify for your own **zip code.**
I *KNEW* I SHOULD HAVE PUT A LOCK ON THE FRIDGE.
NOW YOU HAVE TO LOSE *THREE* POUNDS!
MAYBE I CAN *SLEEP* AWAY A FEW OUNCES...

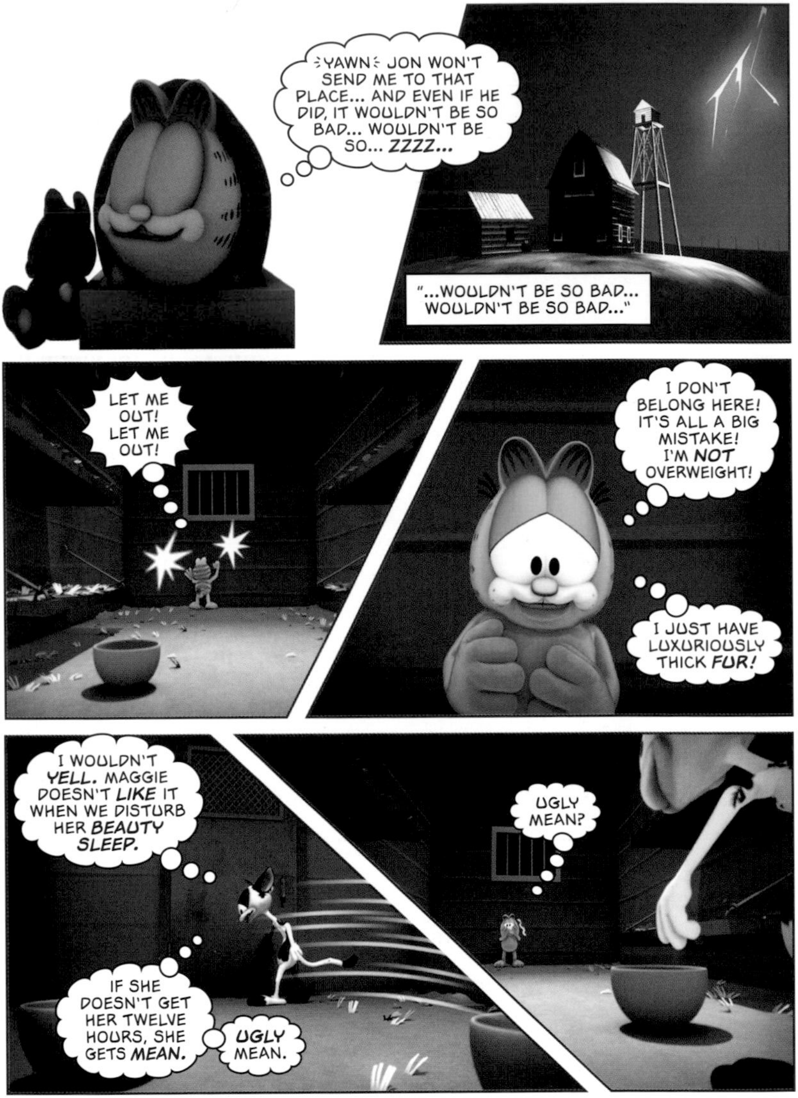

⁼YAWN⁼ JON WON'T SEND ME TO THAT PLACE... AND EVEN IF HE DID, IT WOULDN'T BE SO BAD... WOULDN'T BE SO... ZZZZ...
"...WOULDN'T BE SO BAD... WOULDN'T BE SO BAD..."
LET ME OUT! LET ME OUT!
I DON'T BELONG HERE! IT'S ALL A BIG MISTAKE! I'M NOT OVERWEIGHT!
I JUST HAVE LUXURIOUSLY THICK FUR!
I WOULDN'T YELL. MAGGIE DOESN'T LIKE IT WHEN WE DISTURB HER BEAUTY SLEEP.
IF SHE DOESN'T GET HER TWELVE HOURS, SHE GETS MEAN.
UGLY MEAN.
UGLY MEAN?

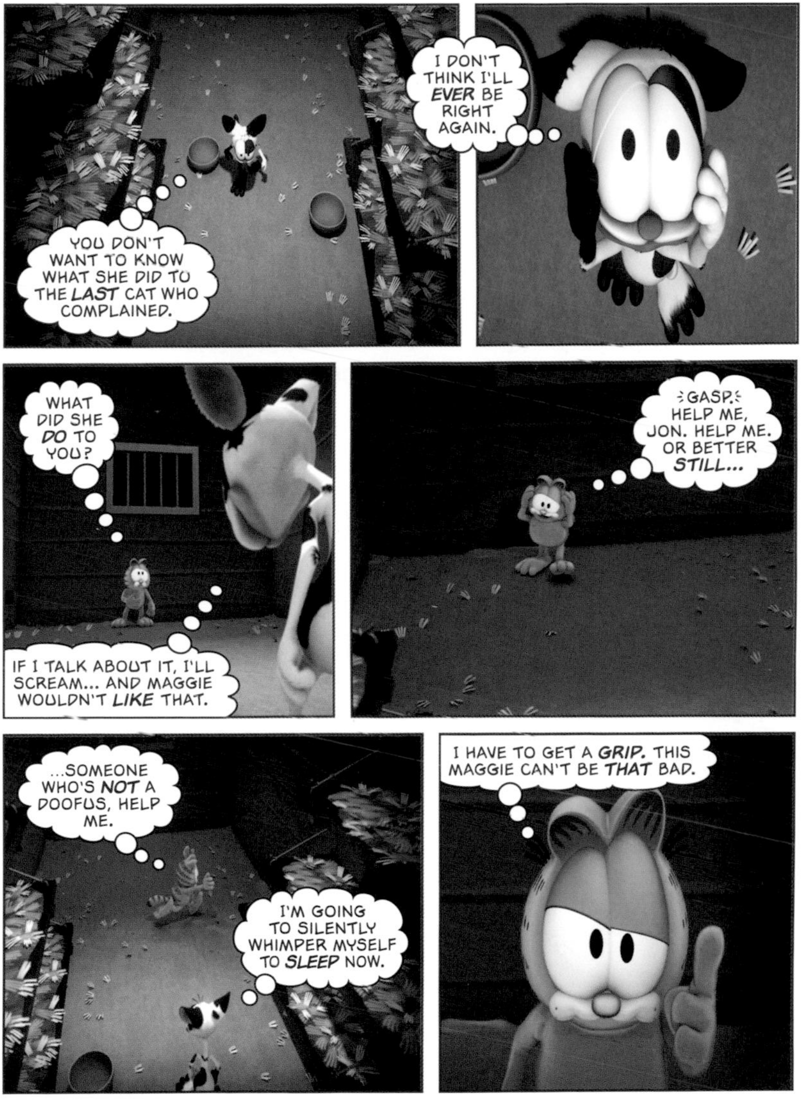
YOU DON'T WANT TO KNOW WHAT SHE DID TO THE LAST CAT WHO COMPLAINED.
I DON'T THINK I'LL EVER BE RIGHT AGAIN.
WHAT DID SHE DO TO YOU?
IF I TALK ABOUT IT, I'LL SCREAM... AND MAGGIE WOULDN'T LIKE THAT.
GASP. HELP ME, JON. HELP ME. OR BETTER STILL...
...SOMEONE WHO'S NOT A DOOFUS, HELP ME.
I'M GOING TO SILENTLY WHIMPER MYSELF TO SLEEP NOW.
I HAVE TO GET A GRIP. THIS MAGGIE CAN'T BE THAT BAD.

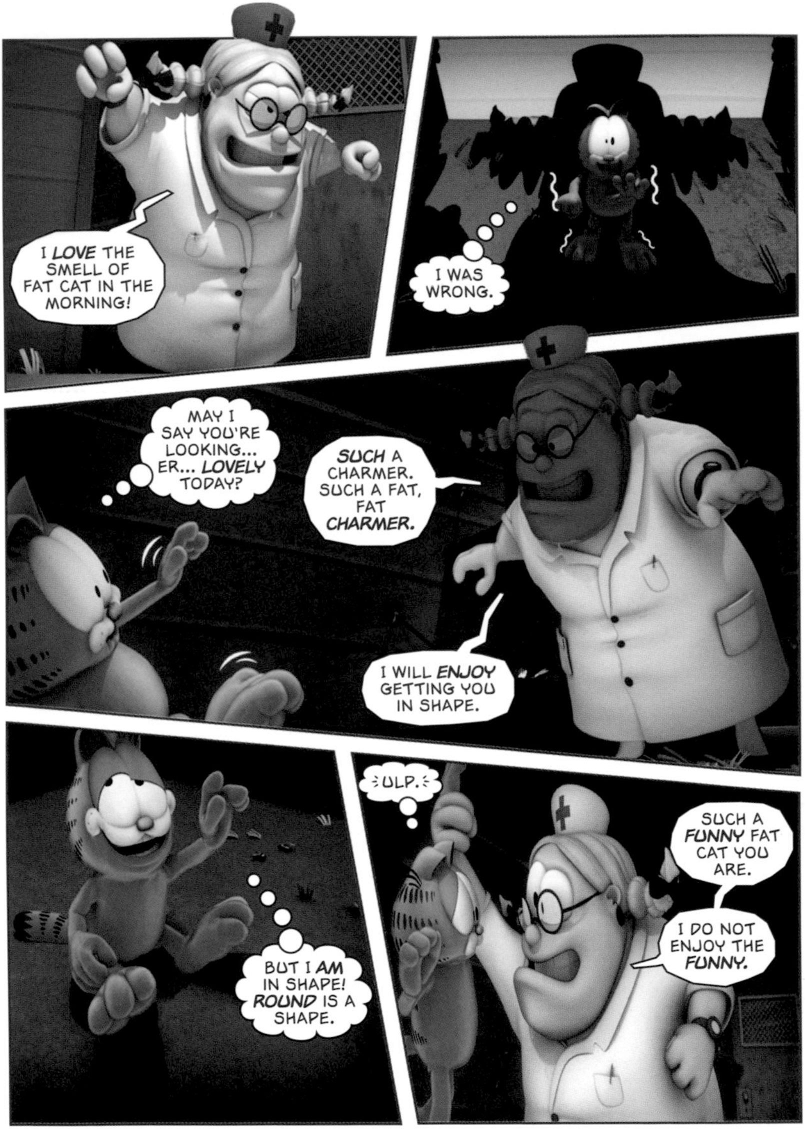
I LOVE THE SMELL OF FAT CAT IN THE MORNING!
I WAS WRONG.
MAY I SAY YOU'RE LOOKING... ER... LOVELY TODAY?
SUCH A CHARMER. SUCH A FAT, FAT CHARMER.
I WILL ENJOY GETTING YOU IN SHAPE.
BUT I AM IN SHAPE! ROUND IS A SHAPE.
ULP.
SUCH A FUNNY FAT CAT YOU ARE.
I DO NOT ENJOY THE FUNNY.

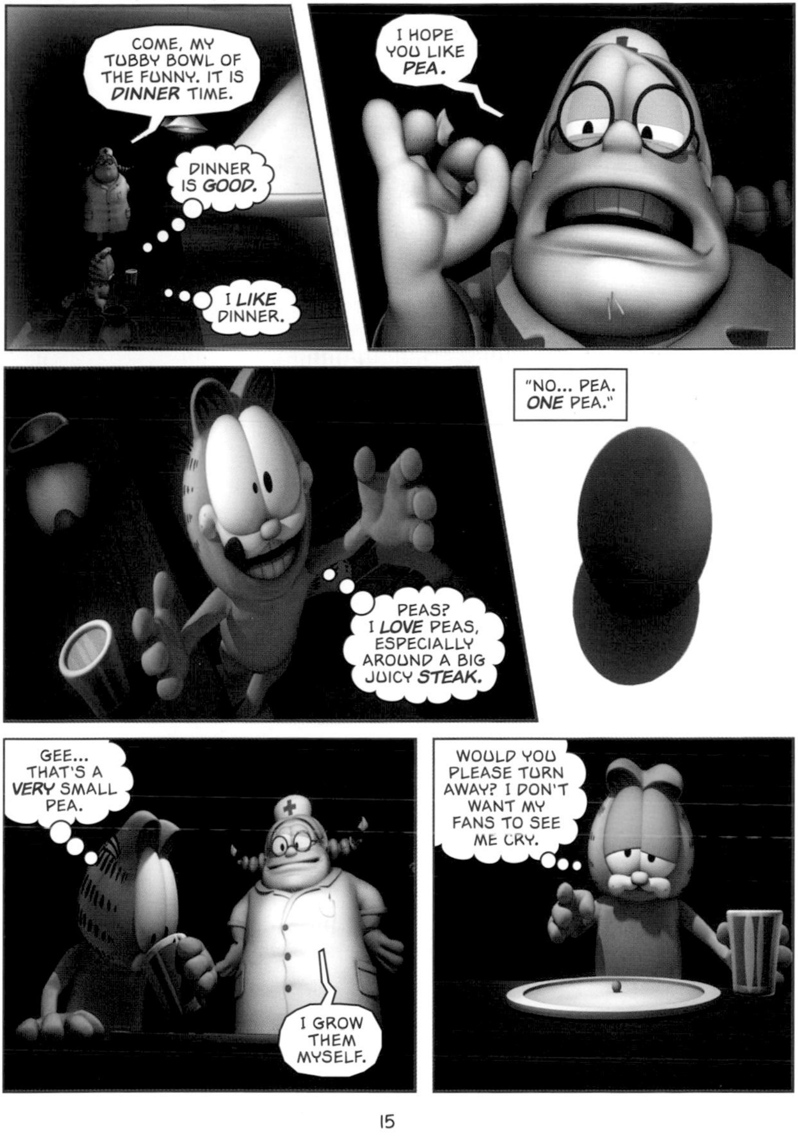
COME, MY TUBBY BOWL OF THE FUNNY. IT IS DINNER TIME.
DINNER IS GOOD.
I LIKE DINNER.
I HOPE YOU LIKE PEA.
PEAS? I LOVE PEAS, ESPECIALLY AROUND A BIG JUICY STEAK.
"NO... PEA. ONE PEA."
GEE... THAT'S A VERY SMALL PEA.
I GROW THEM MYSELF.
WOULD YOU PLEASE TURN AWAY? I DON'T WANT MY FANS TO SEE ME CRY.

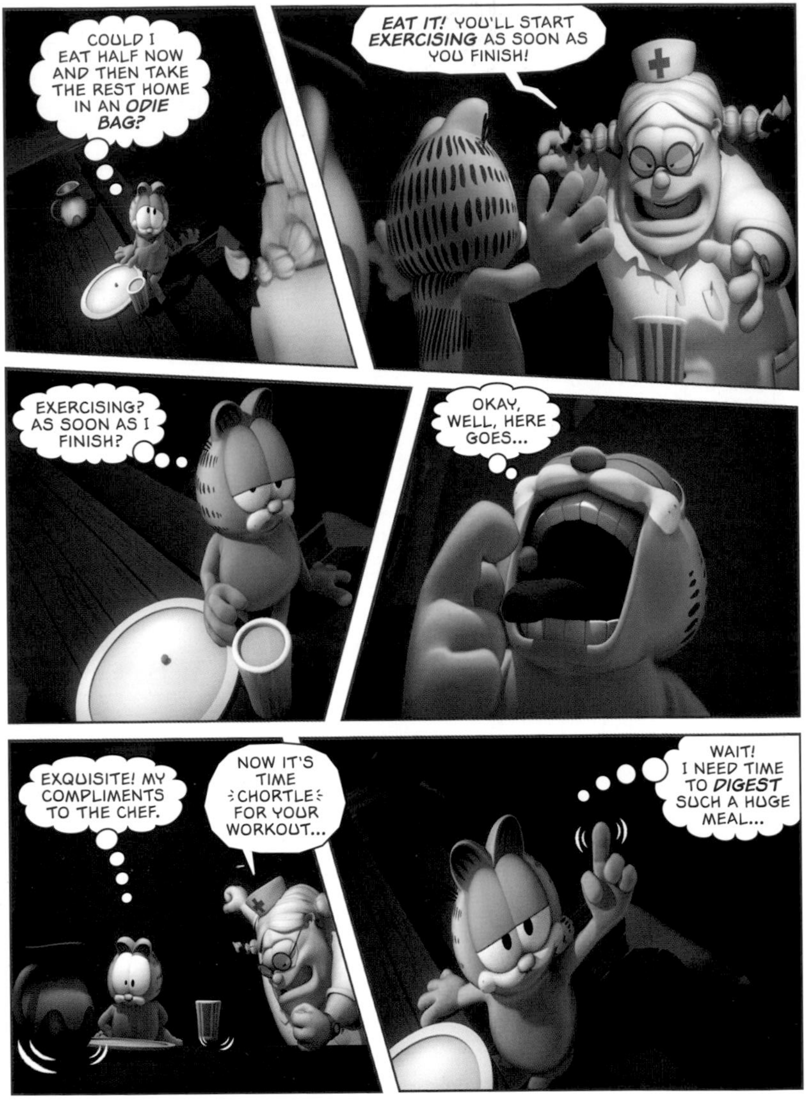
COULD I EAT HALF NOW AND THEN TAKE THE REST HOME IN AN ODIE BAG?
EAT IT! YOU'LL START EXERCISING AS SOON AS YOU FINISH!
EXERCISING? AS SOON AS I FINISH?
OKAY, WELL, HERE GOES...
EXQUISITE! MY COMPLIMENTS TO THE CHEF.
NOW IT'S TIME ⁝CHORTLE⁝ FOR YOUR WORKOUT...
WAIT! I NEED TIME TO DIGEST SUCH A HUGE MEAL...

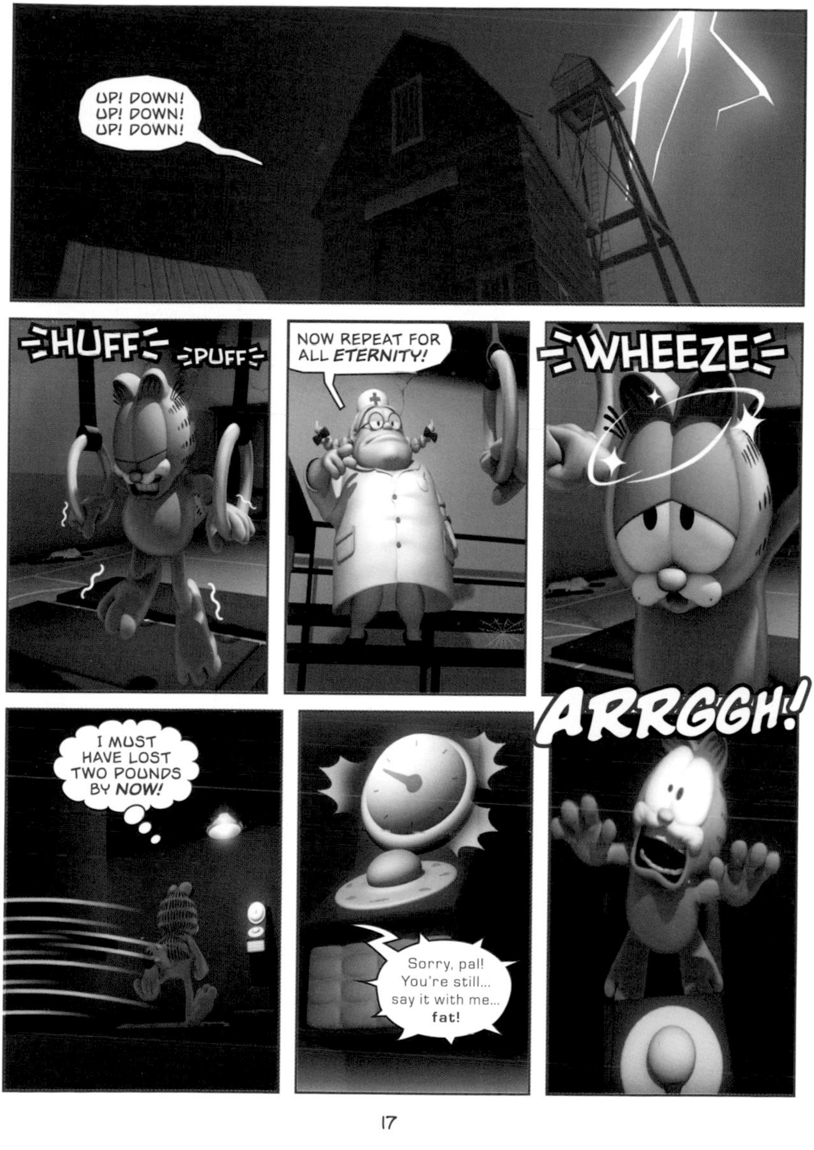
UP! DOWN!
UP! DOWN!
UP! DOWN!
HUFF
PUFF
NOW REPEAT FOR ALL *ETERNITY!*
WHEEZE
I MUST HAVE LOST TWO POUNDS BY *NOW!*
Sorry, pal! You're still... say it with me... **fat!**
ARRGGH!

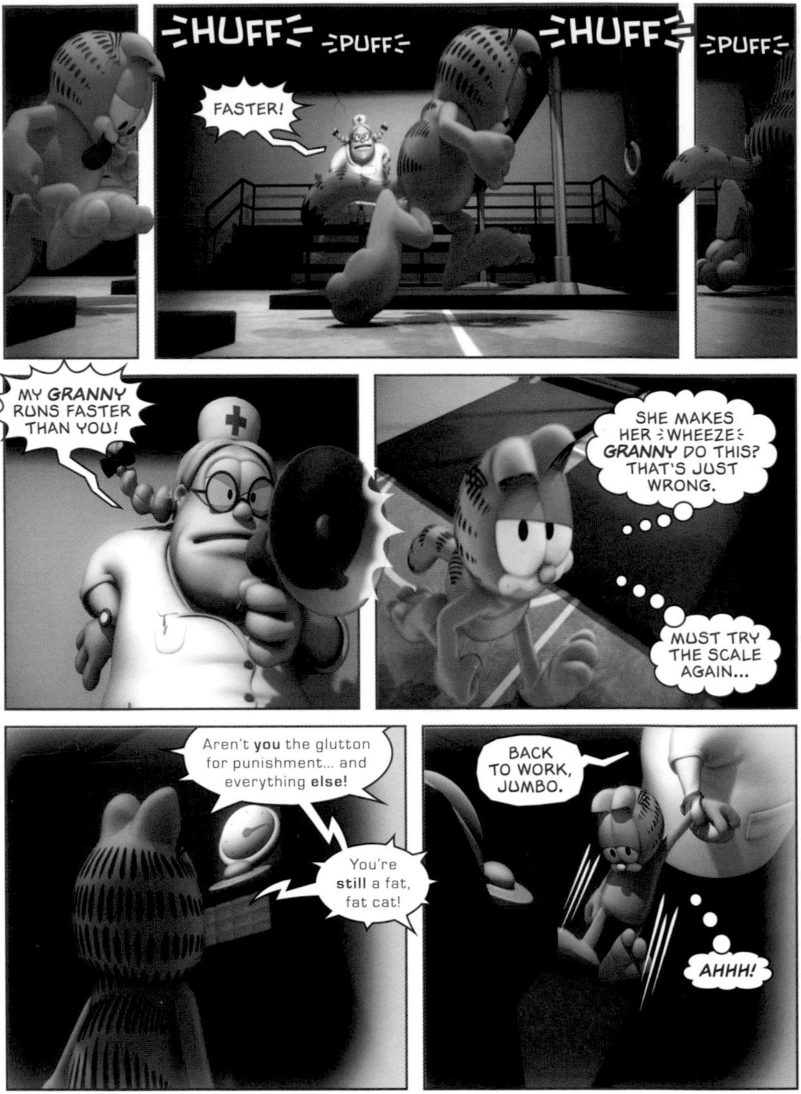
HUFF
PUFF
FASTER!
HUFF
PUFF
MY GRANNY RUNS FASTER THAN YOU!
SHE MAKES HER WHEEZE GRANNY DO THIS? THAT'S JUST WRONG.
MUST TRY THE SCALE AGAIN...
Aren't you the glutton for punishment... and everything else!
You're still a fat, fat cat!
BACK TO WORK, JUMBO.
AHHH!

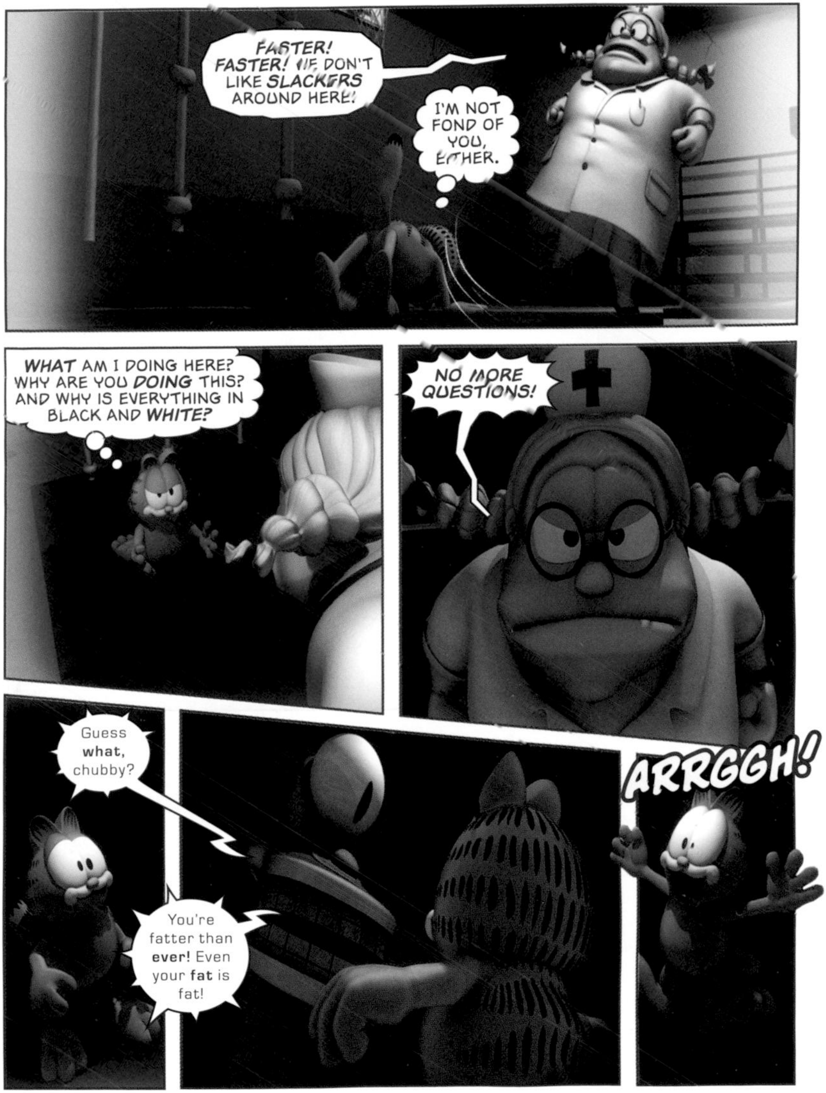

FASTER! FASTER! WE DON'T LIKE SLACKERS AROUND HERE!
I'M NOT FOND OF YOU, EITHER.
WHAT AM I DOING HERE? WHY ARE YOU DOING THIS? AND WHY IS EVERYTHING IN BLACK AND WHITE?
NO MORE QUESTIONS!
Guess what, chubby?
You're fatter than ever! Even your fat is fat!
ARRGGH!

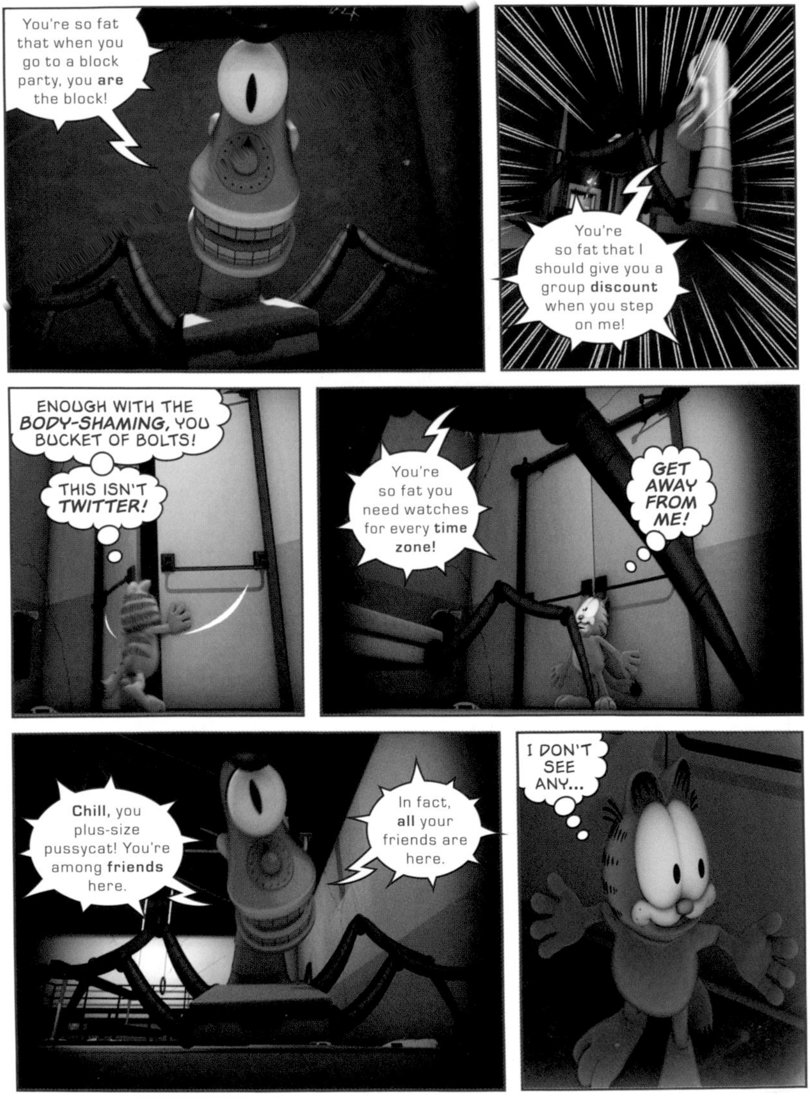
You're so fat that when you go to a block party, you **are** the block!
You're so fat that I should give you a group **discount** when you step on me!
ENOUGH WITH THE *BODY-SHAMING,* YOU BUCKET OF BOLTS!
THIS ISN'T *TWITTER!*
You're so fat you need watches for every **time zone!**
GET AWAY FROM ME!
Chill, you plus-size pussycat! You're among **friends** here.
In fact, **all** your friends are here.
I DON'T SEE ANY...

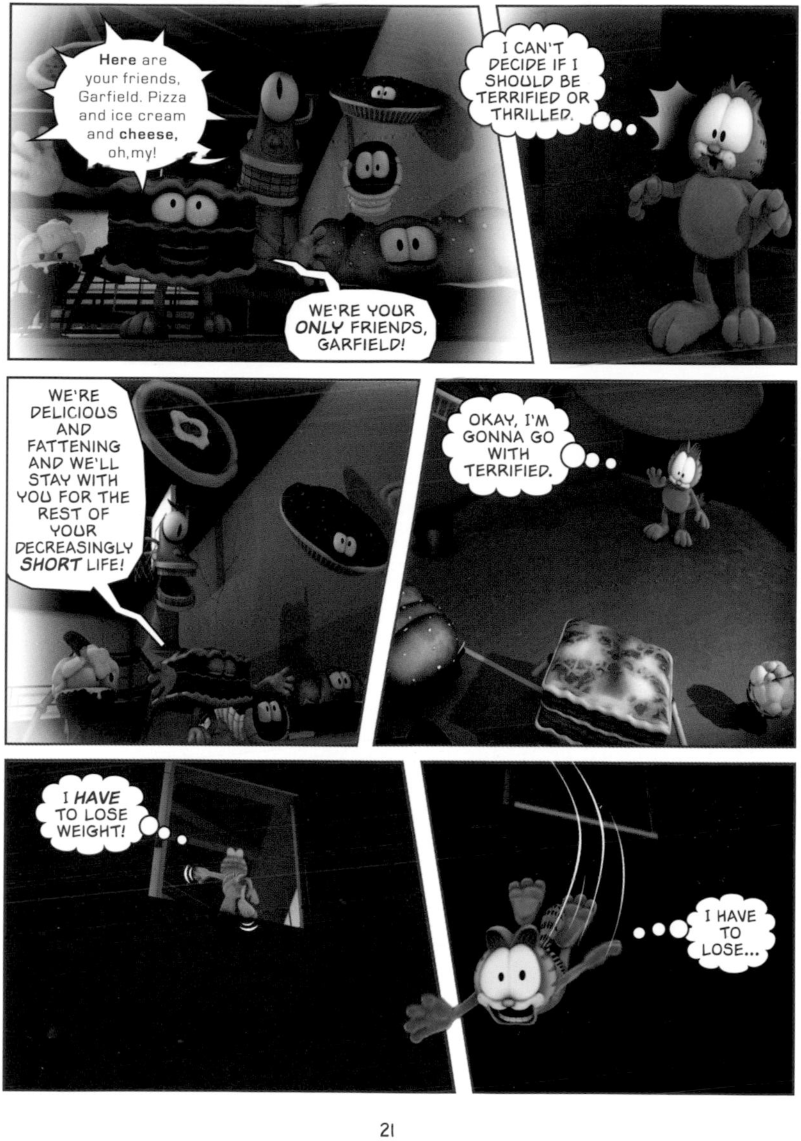

Here are your friends, Garfield. Pizza and ice cream and cheese, oh,my!
I CAN'T DECIDE IF I SHOULD BE TERRIFIED OR THRILLED.
WE'RE YOUR ONLY FRIENDS, GARFIELD!
WE'RE DELICIOUS AND FATTENING AND WE'LL STAY WITH YOU FOR THE REST OF YOUR DECREASINGLY SHORT LIFE!
OKAY, I'M GONNA GO WITH TERRIFIED.
I HAVE TO LOSE WEIGHT!
I HAVE TO LOSE...

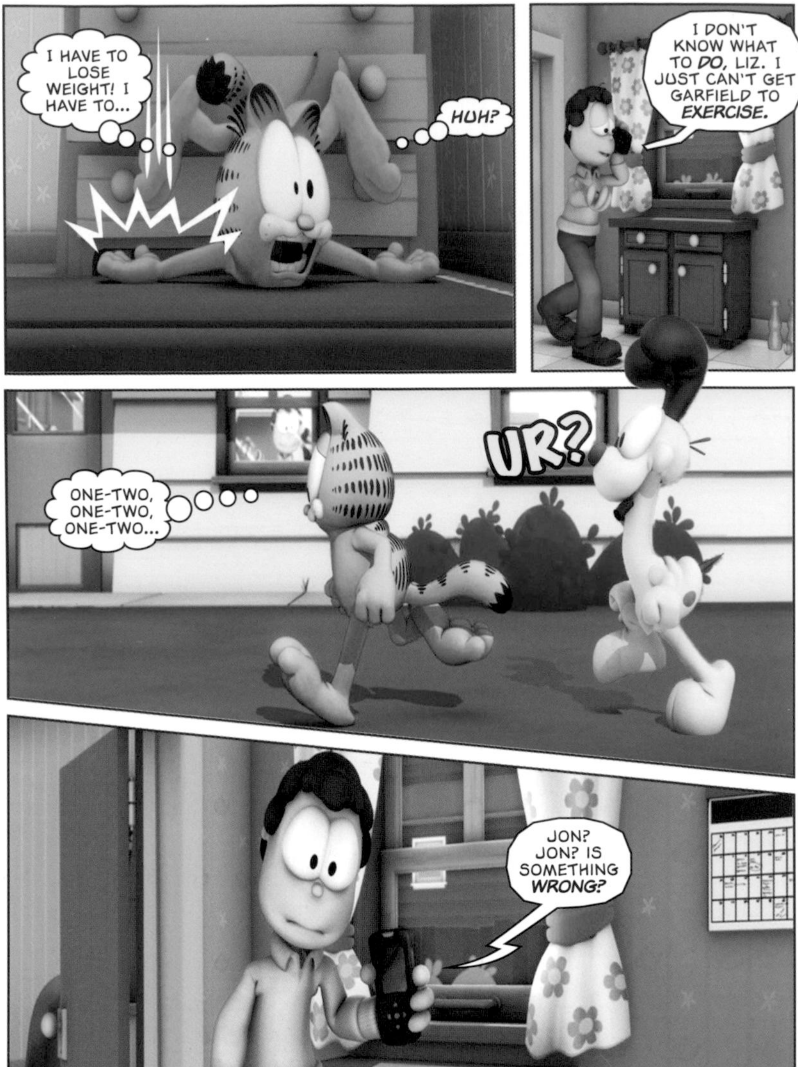
I HAVE TO LOSE WEIGHT! I HAVE TO...
HUH?
I DON'T KNOW WHAT TO DO, LIZ. I JUST CAN'T GET GARFIELD TO EXERCISE.
UR?
ONE-TWO, ONE-TWO, ONE-TWO...
JON? JON? IS SOMETHING WRONG?

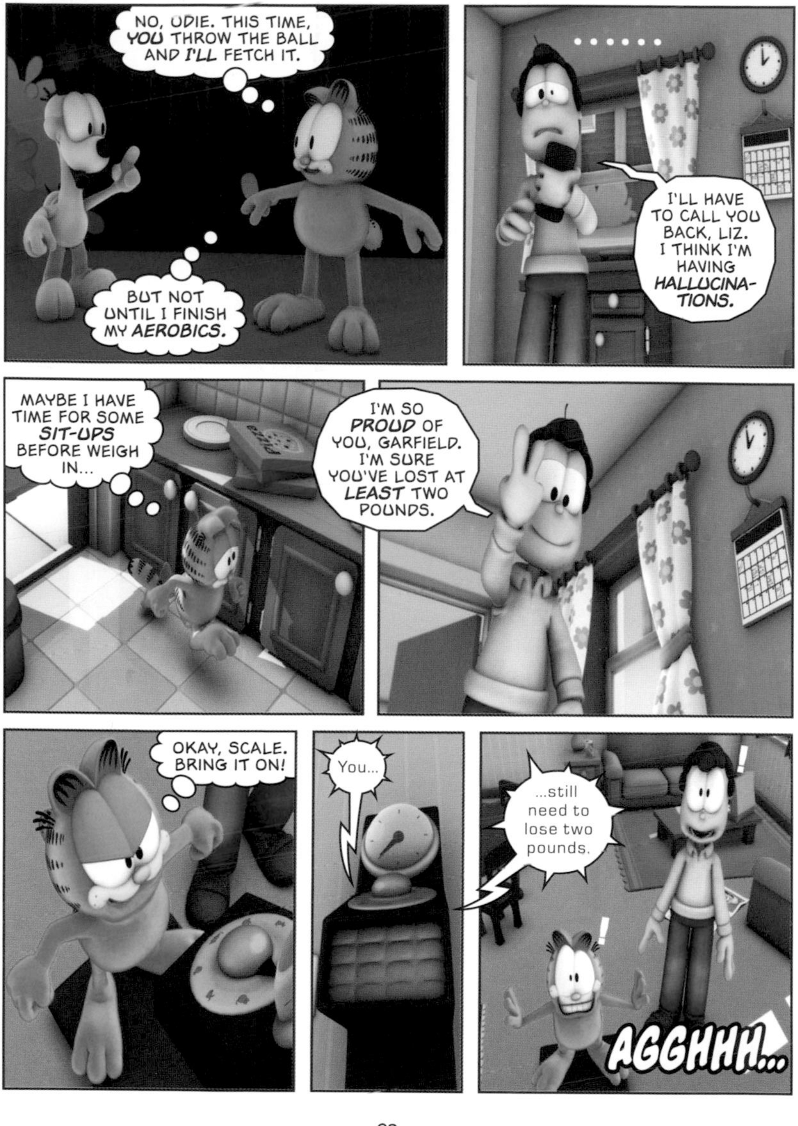
NO, ODIE. THIS TIME, YOU THROW THE BALL AND I'LL FETCH IT.
BUT NOT UNTIL I FINISH MY AEROBICS.
• • • • • • •
I'LL HAVE TO CALL YOU BACK, LIZ. I THINK I'M HAVING HALLUCINATIONS.
MAYBE I HAVE TIME FOR SOME SIT-UPS BEFORE WEIGH IN...
I'M SO PROUD OF YOU, GARFIELD. I'M SURE YOU'VE LOST AT LEAST TWO POUNDS.
OKAY, SCALE. BRING IT ON!
You...
...still need to lose two pounds.
AGGHHH...

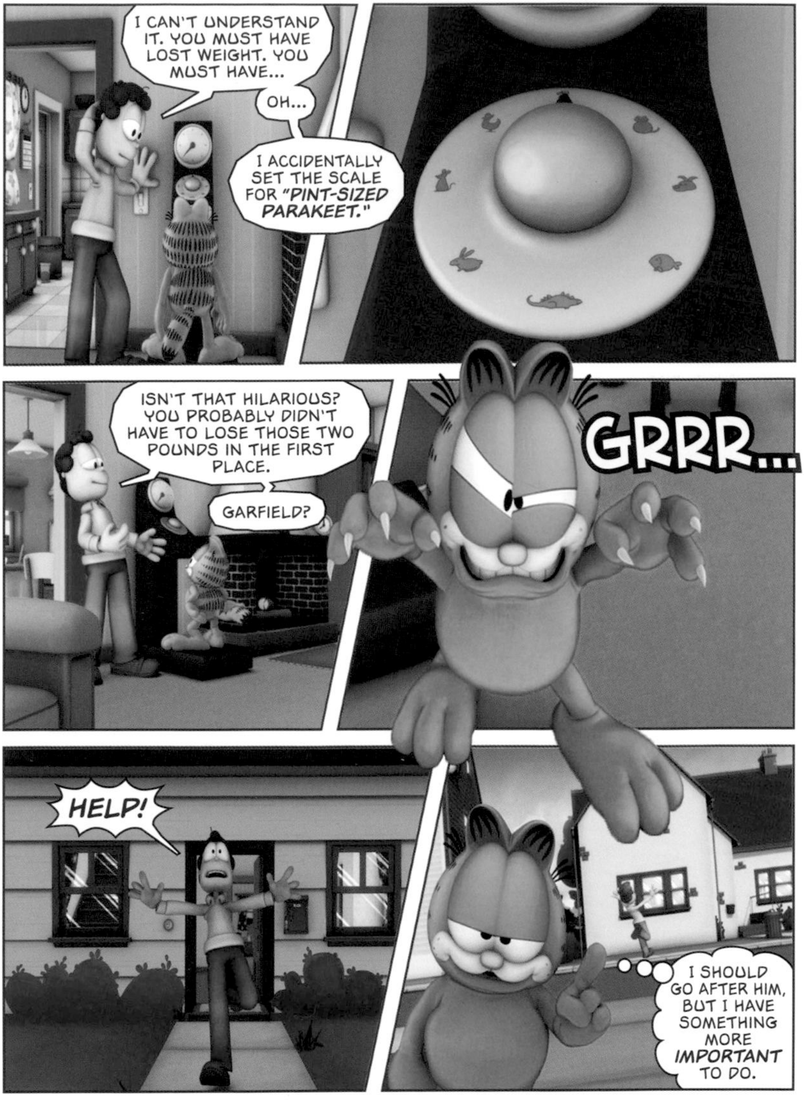
I CAN'T UNDERSTAND IT. YOU MUST HAVE LOST WEIGHT. YOU MUST HAVE...
OH...
I ACCIDENTALLY SET THE SCALE FOR "PINT-SIZED PARAKEET."
ISN'T THAT HILARIOUS? YOU PROBABLY DIDN'T HAVE TO LOSE THOSE TWO POUNDS IN THE FIRST PLACE.
GARFIELD?
GRRR...
HELP!
I SHOULD GO AFTER HIM, BUT I HAVE SOMETHING MORE IMPORTANT TO DO.

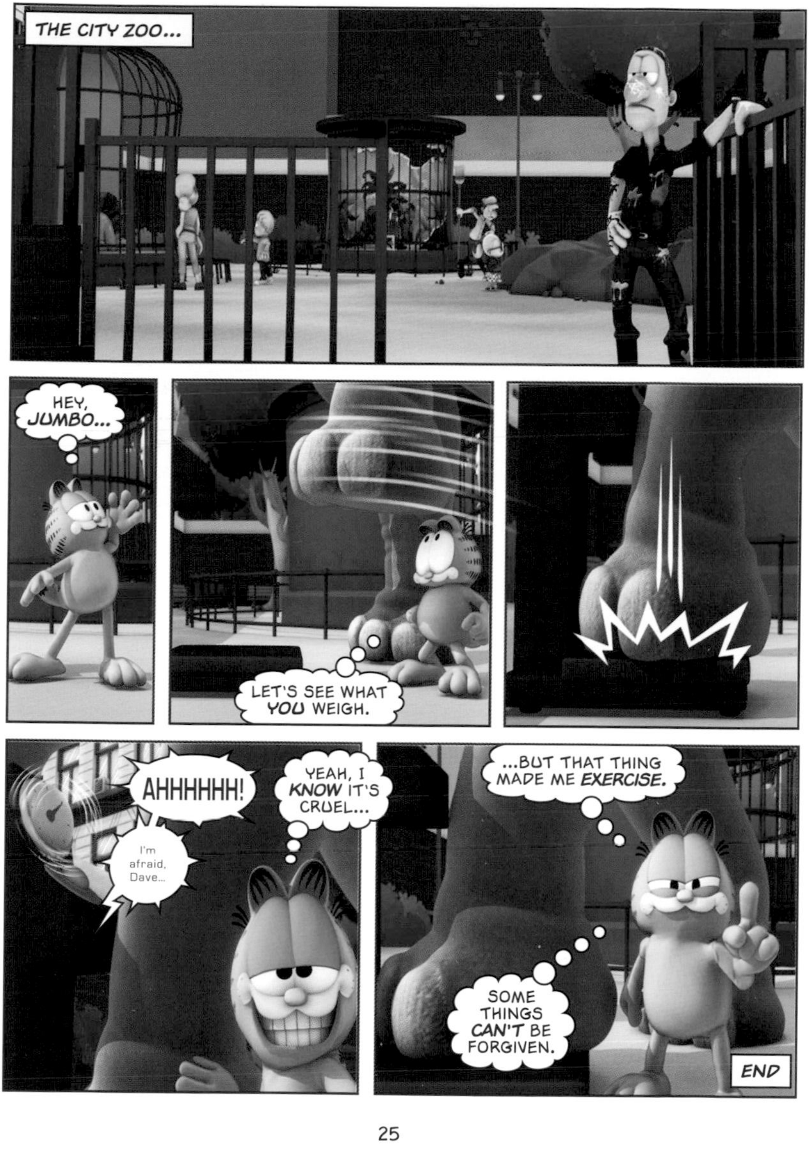
THE CITY ZOO...
HEY, JUMBO...
LET'S SEE WHAT YOU WEIGH.
AHHHHHH!
I'm afraid, Dave...
YEAH, I KNOW IT'S CRUEL...
...BUT THAT THING MADE ME EXERCISE.
SOME THINGS CAN'T BE FORGIVEN.
END

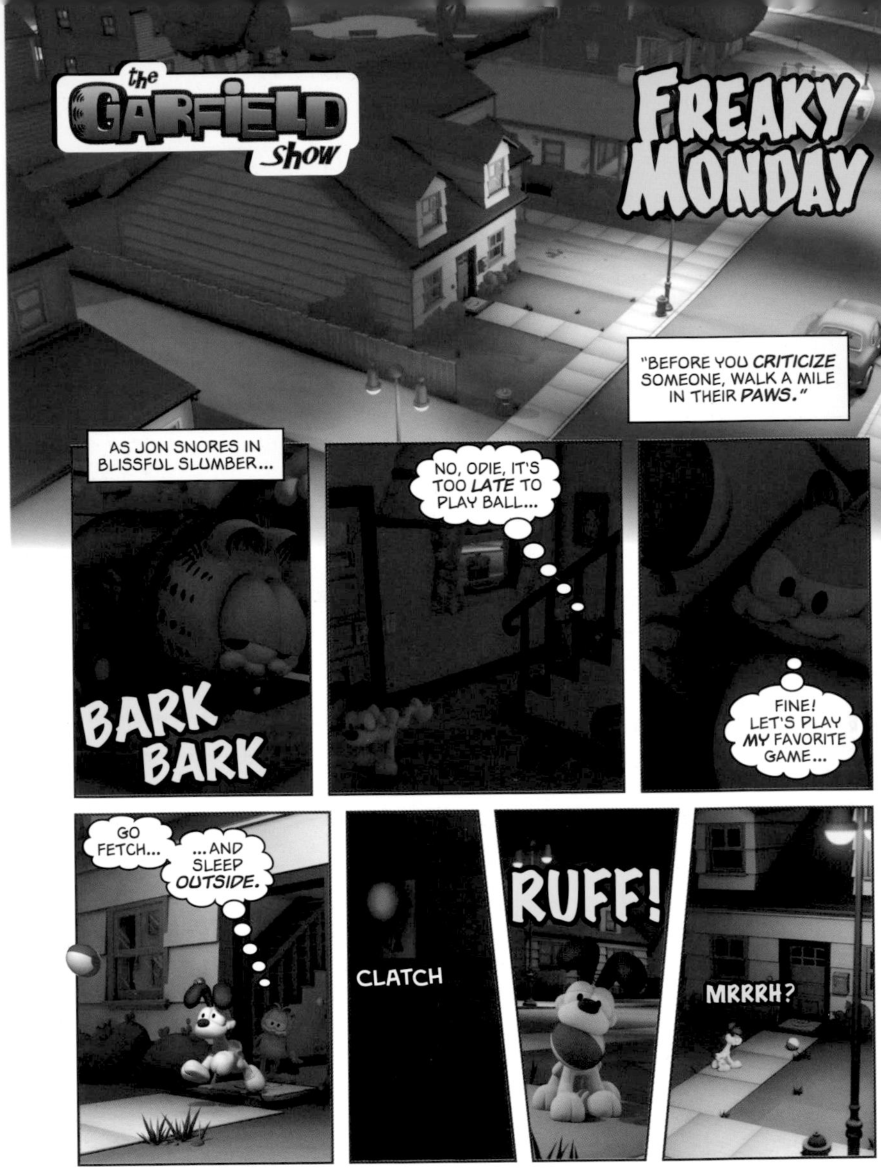
the GARFIELD show
FREAKY MONDAY
"BEFORE YOU CRITICIZE SOMEONE, WALK A MILE IN THEIR PAWS."
AS JON SNORES IN BLISSFUL SLUMBER...
BARK BARK
NO, ODIE, IT'S TOO LATE TO PLAY BALL...
FINE! LET'S PLAY MY FAVORITE GAME...
GO FETCH...
...AND SLEEP OUTSIDE.
CLATCH
RUFF!
MRRRH?

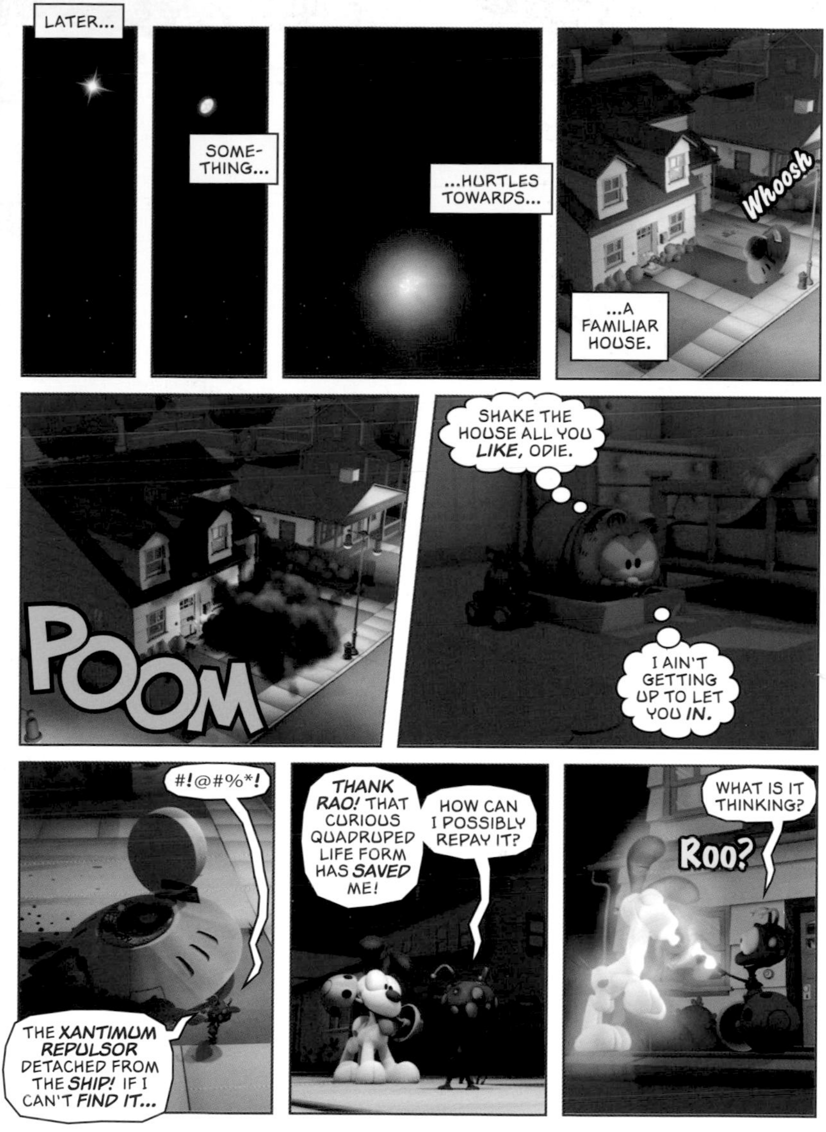

LATER...
SOME-THING...
...HURTLES TOWARDS...
...A FAMILIAR HOUSE.
Whoosh
POOM
SHAKE THE HOUSE ALL YOU *LIKE,* ODIE.
I AIN'T GETTING UP TO LET YOU *IN.*
#!@#%*!
THE *XANTIMUM REPULSOR* DETACHED FROM THE *SHIP!* IF I CAN'T *FIND IT...*
THANK RAO! THAT CURIOUS QUADRUPED LIFE FORM HAS *SAVED* ME!
HOW CAN I POSSIBLY REPAY IT?
WHAT IS IT THINKING?
Roo?

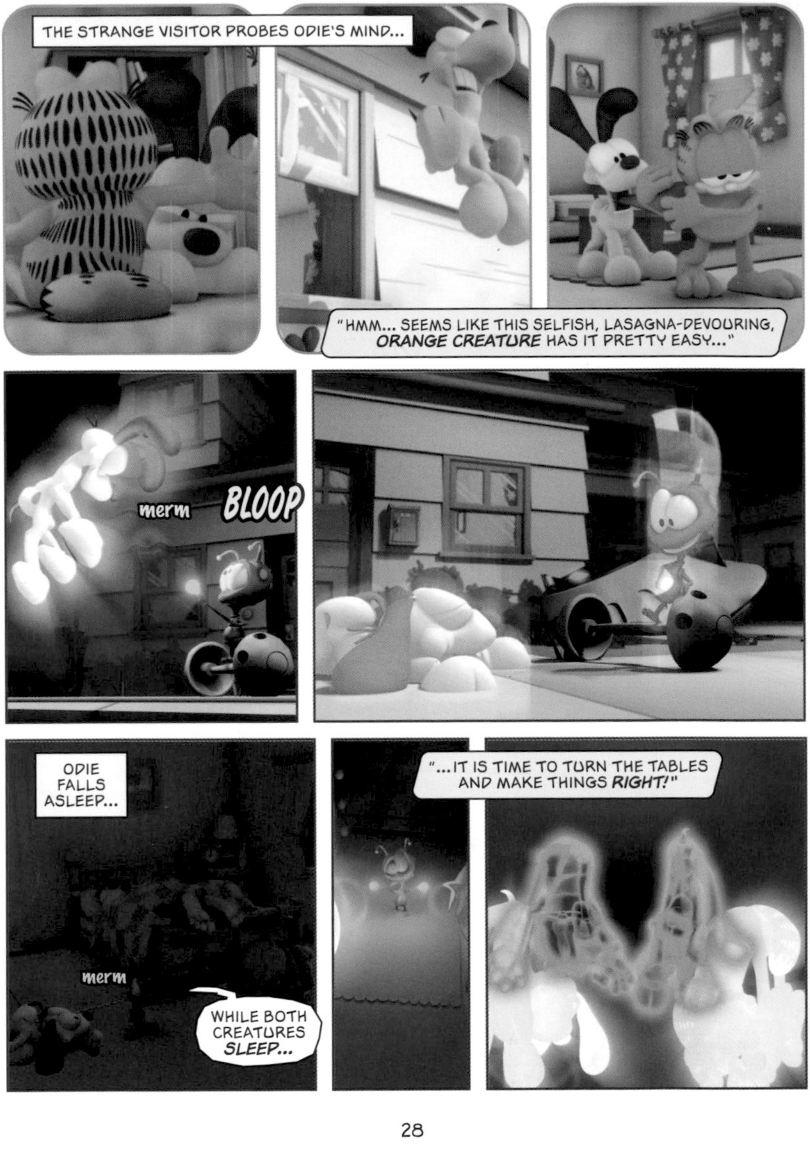
THE STRANGE VISITOR PROBES ODIE'S MIND...
"HMM... SEEMS LIKE THIS SELFISH, LASAGNA-DEVOURING, ORANGE CREATURE HAS IT PRETTY EASY..."
merm
BLOOP
ODIE FALLS ASLEEP...
merm
WHILE BOTH CREATURES SLEEP...
"...IT IS TIME TO TURN THE TABLES AND MAKE THINGS RIGHT!"

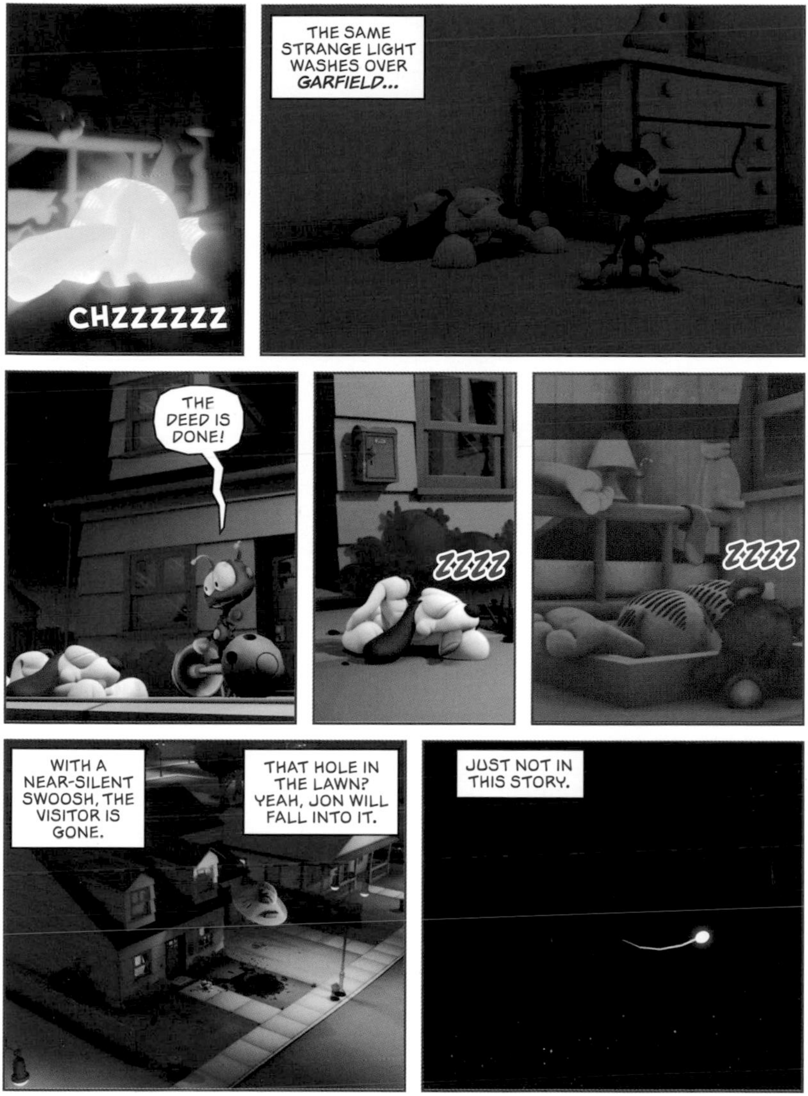
CHZZZZZZ
THE SAME STRANGE LIGHT WASHES OVER *GARFIELD*...
THE DEED IS DONE!
ZZZZ
ZZZZ
WITH A NEAR-SILENT SWOOSH, THE VISITOR IS GONE.
THAT HOLE IN THE LAWN? YEAH, JON WILL FALL INTO IT.
JUST NOT IN THIS STORY.

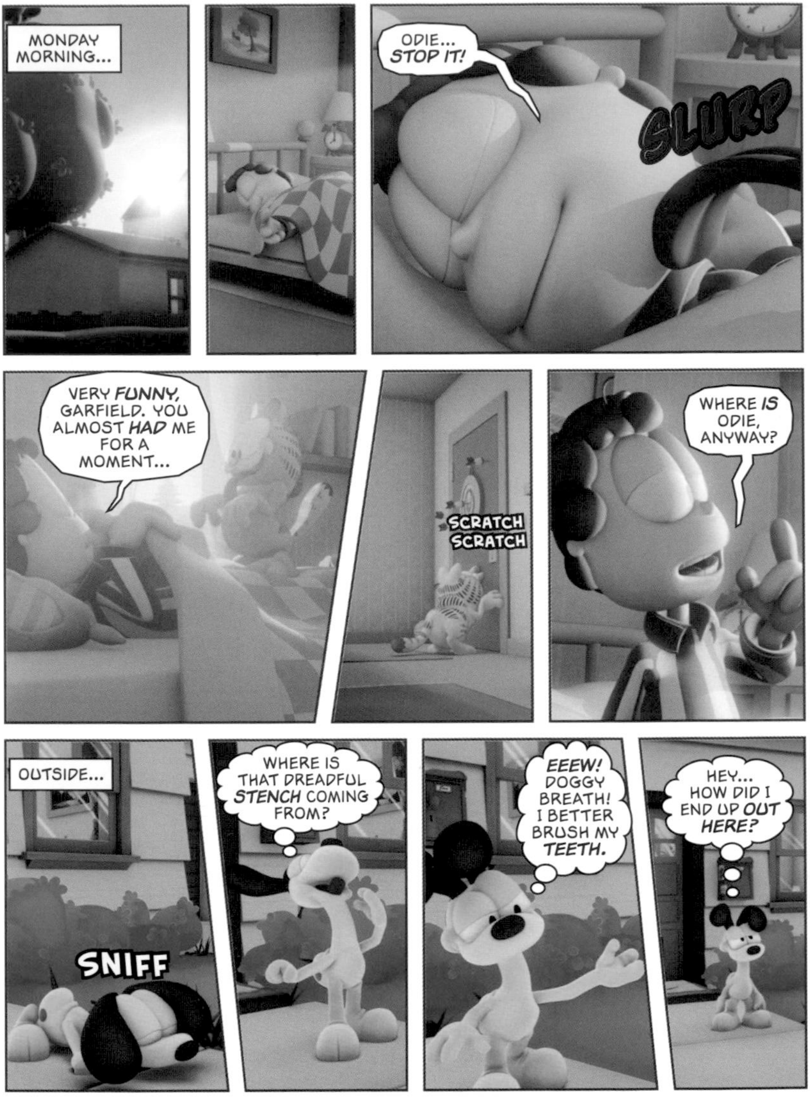
MONDAY MORNING...
ODIE... STOP IT!
SLURP
VERY FUNNY, GARFIELD. YOU ALMOST HAD ME FOR A MOMENT...
SCRATCH SCRATCH
WHERE IS ODIE, ANYWAY?
OUTSIDE...
SNIFF
WHERE IS THAT DREADFUL STENCH COMING FROM?
EEEW! DOGGY BREATH! I BETTER BRUSH MY TEETH.
HEY... HOW DID I END UP OUT HERE?

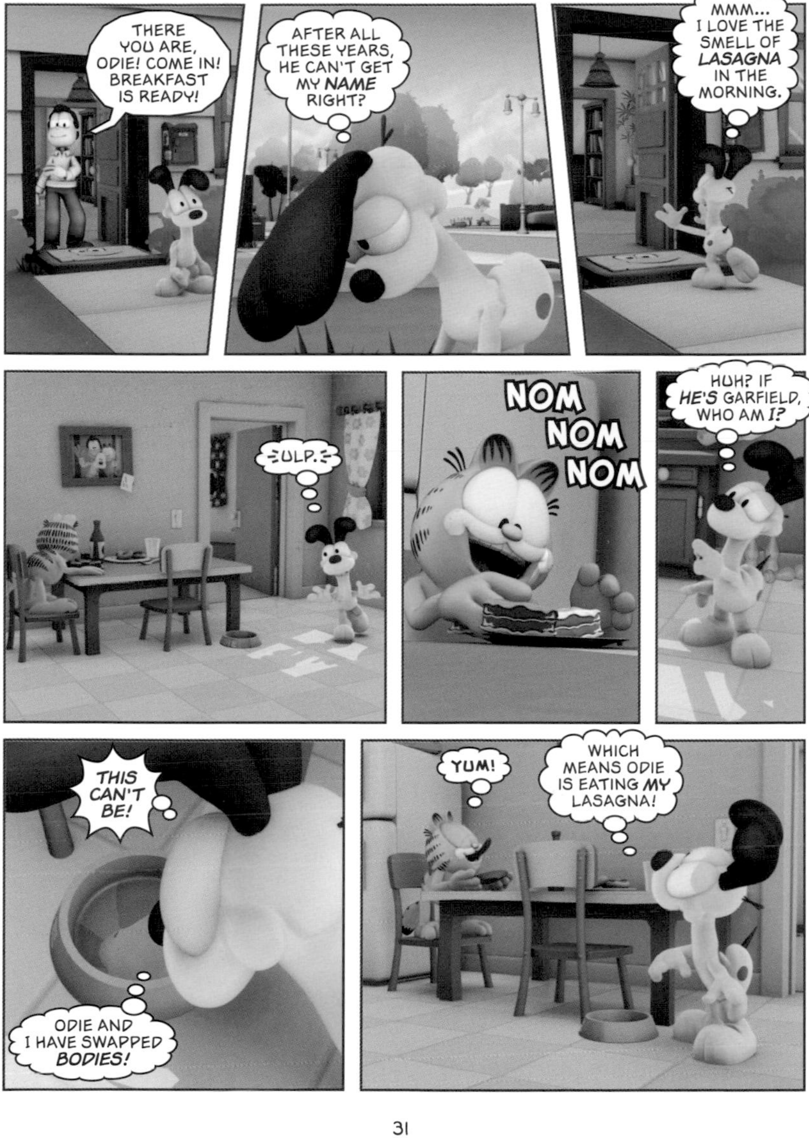
THERE YOU ARE, ODIE! COME IN! BREAKFAST IS READY!
AFTER ALL THESE YEARS, HE CAN'T GET MY NAME RIGHT?
MMM... I LOVE THE SMELL OF LASAGNA IN THE MORNING.
ULP.
NOM NOM NOM
HUH? IF HE'S GARFIELD, WHO AM I?
THIS CAN'T BE!
ODIE AND I HAVE SWAPPED BODIES!
YUM!
WHICH MEANS ODIE IS EATING MY LASAGNA!

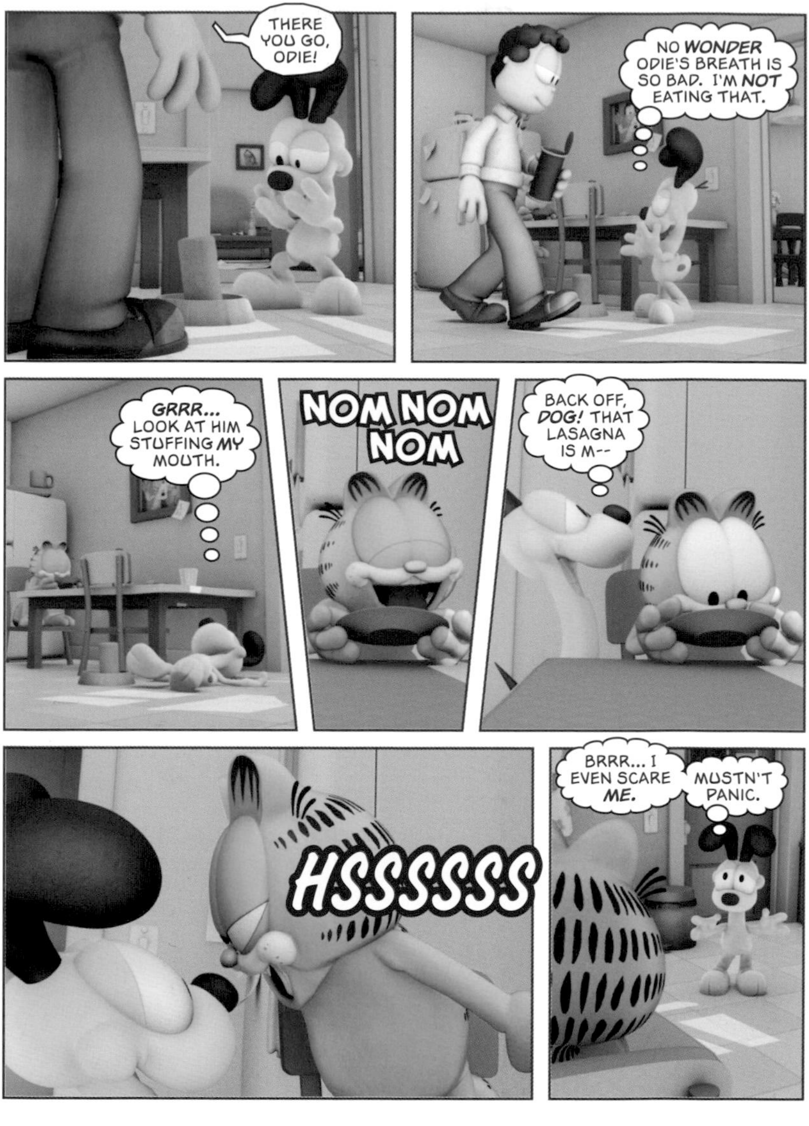
THERE YOU GO, ODIE!
NO WONDER ODIE'S BREATH IS SO BAD. I'M NOT EATING THAT.
GRRR... LOOK AT HIM STUFFING MY MOUTH.
NOM NOM NOM
BACK OFF, DOG! THAT LASAGNA IS M--
HSSSSSS
BRRR... I EVEN SCARE ME.
MUSTN'T PANIC.

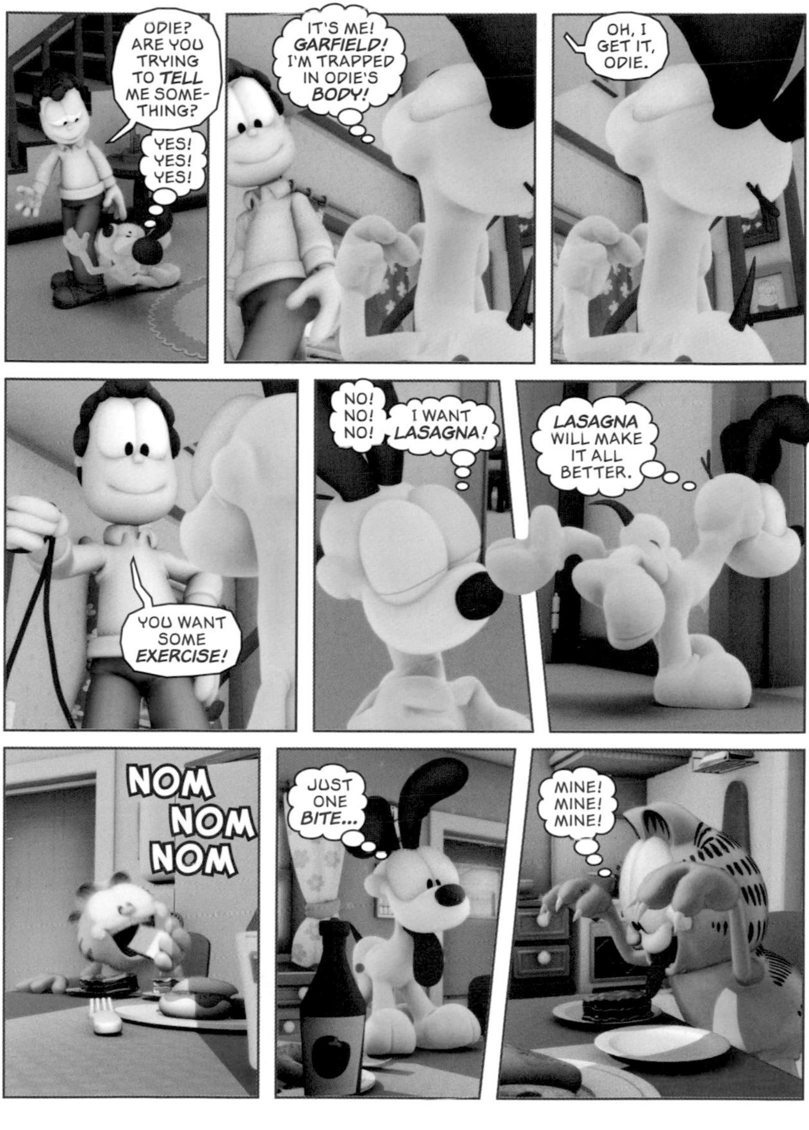
ODIE? ARE YOU TRYING TO TELL ME SOMETHING?
YES! YES! YES!
IT'S ME! GARFIELD! I'M TRAPPED IN ODIE'S BODY!
OH, I GET IT, ODIE.
YOU WANT SOME EXERCISE!
NO! NO! NO!
I WANT LASAGNA!
LASAGNA WILL MAKE IT ALL BETTER.
NOM NOM NOM
JUST ONE BITE...
MINE! MINE! MINE!

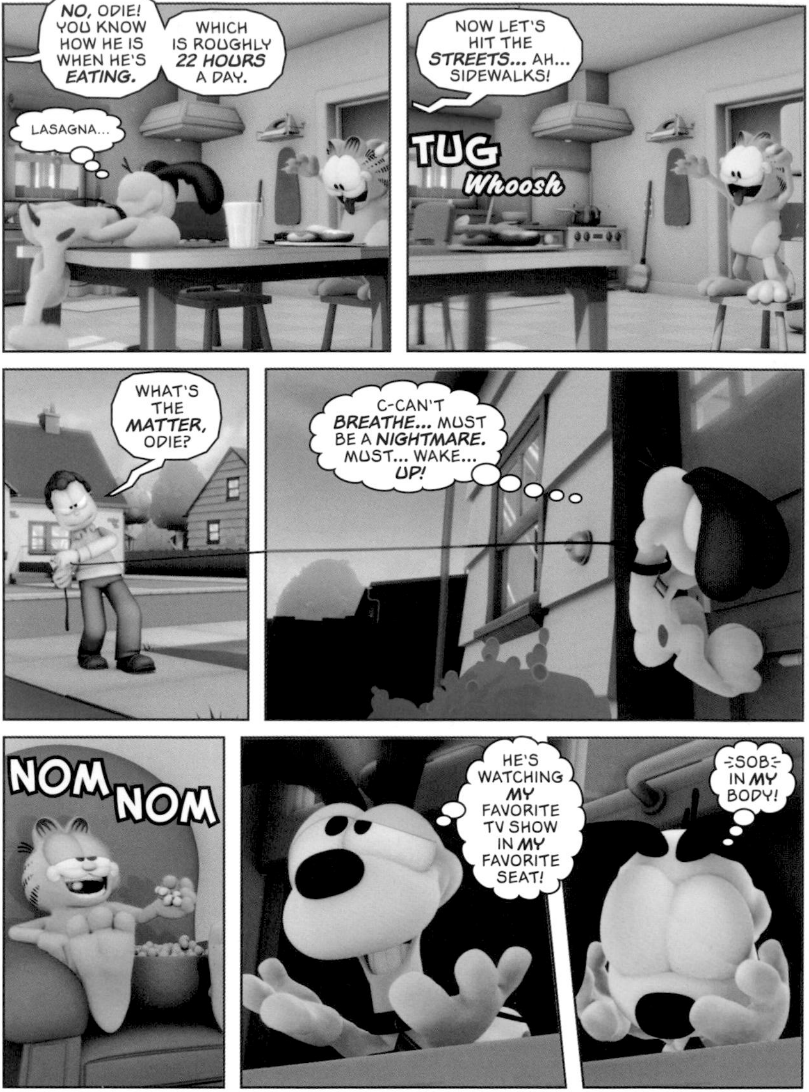
NO, ODIE! YOU KNOW HOW HE IS WHEN HE'S EATING.
WHICH IS ROUGHLY 22 HOURS A DAY.
LASAGNA...
NOW LET'S HIT THE STREETS... AH... SIDEWALKS!
TUG
Whoosh
WHAT'S THE MATTER, ODIE?
C-CAN'T BREATHE... MUST BE A NIGHTMARE. MUST... WAKE... UP!
NOM NOM
HE'S WATCHING MY FAVORITE TV SHOW IN MY FAVORITE SEAT!
SOB IN MY BODY!

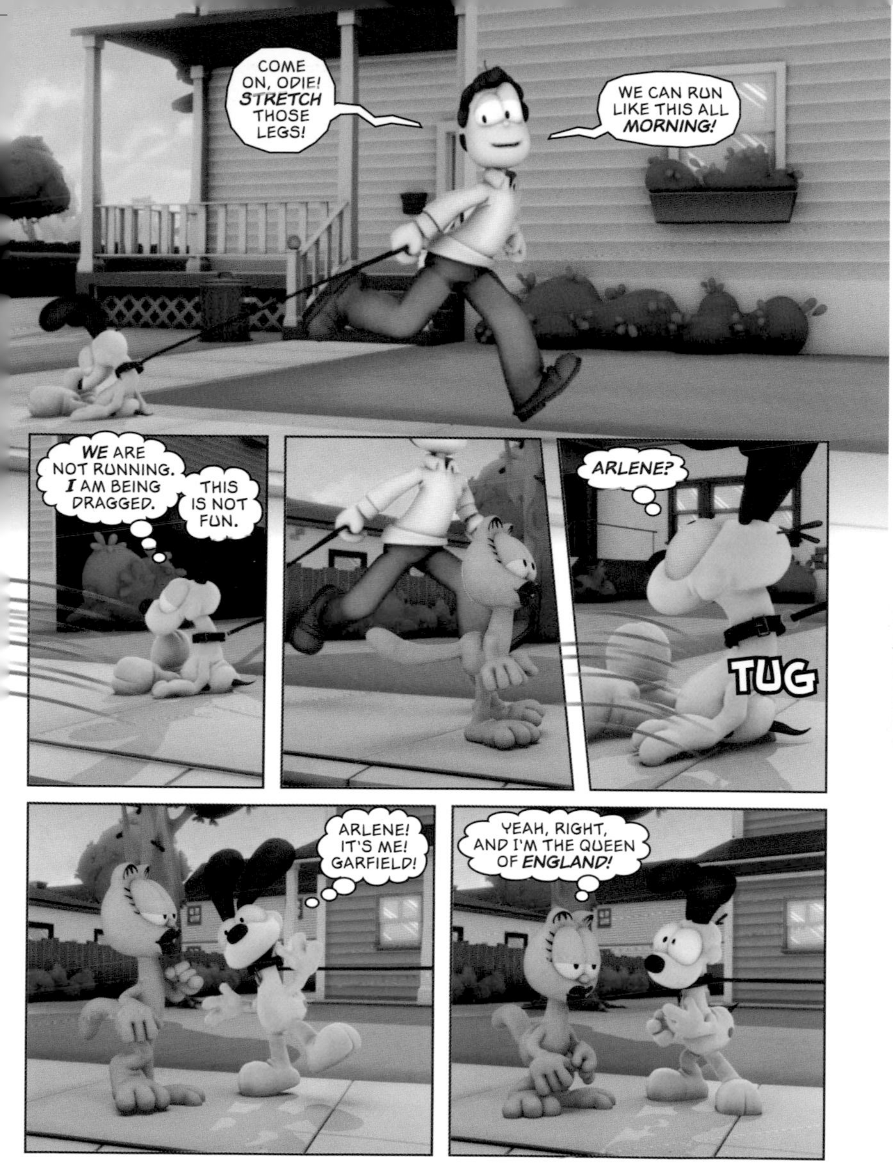
COME ON, ODIE! STRETCH THOSE LEGS!
WE CAN RUN LIKE THIS ALL MORNING!
WE ARE NOT RUNNING. I AM BEING DRAGGED.
THIS IS NOT FUN.
ARLENE?
TUG
ARLENE! IT'S ME! GARFIELD!
YEAH, RIGHT, AND I'M THE QUEEN OF ENGLAND!

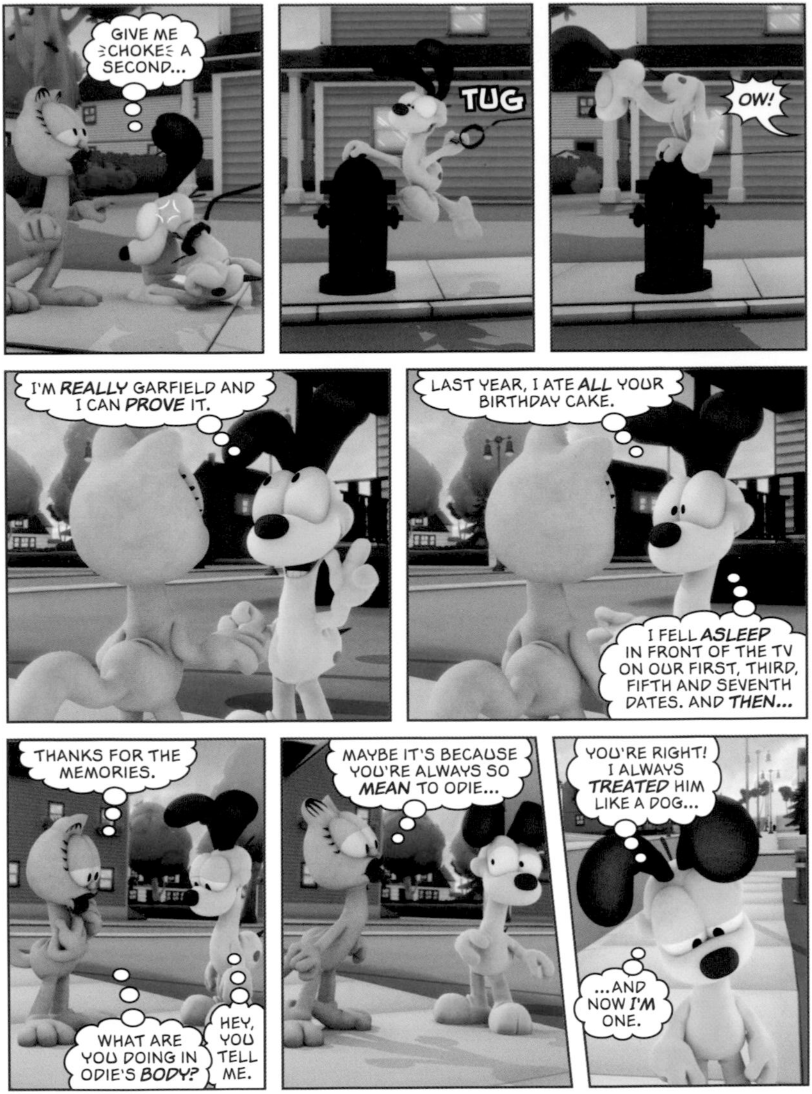
GIVE ME ≷CHOKE≷ A SECOND...
TUG
OW!
I'M REALLY GARFIELD AND I CAN PROVE IT.
LAST YEAR, I ATE ALL YOUR BIRTHDAY CAKE.
I FELL ASLEEP IN FRONT OF THE TV ON OUR FIRST, THIRD, FIFTH AND SEVENTH DATES. AND THEN...
THANKS FOR THE MEMORIES.
WHAT ARE YOU DOING IN ODIE'S BODY?
HEY, YOU TELL ME.
MAYBE IT'S BECAUSE YOU'RE ALWAYS SO MEAN TO ODIE...
YOU'RE RIGHT! I ALWAYS TREATED HIM LIKE A DOG...
...AND NOW I'M ONE.

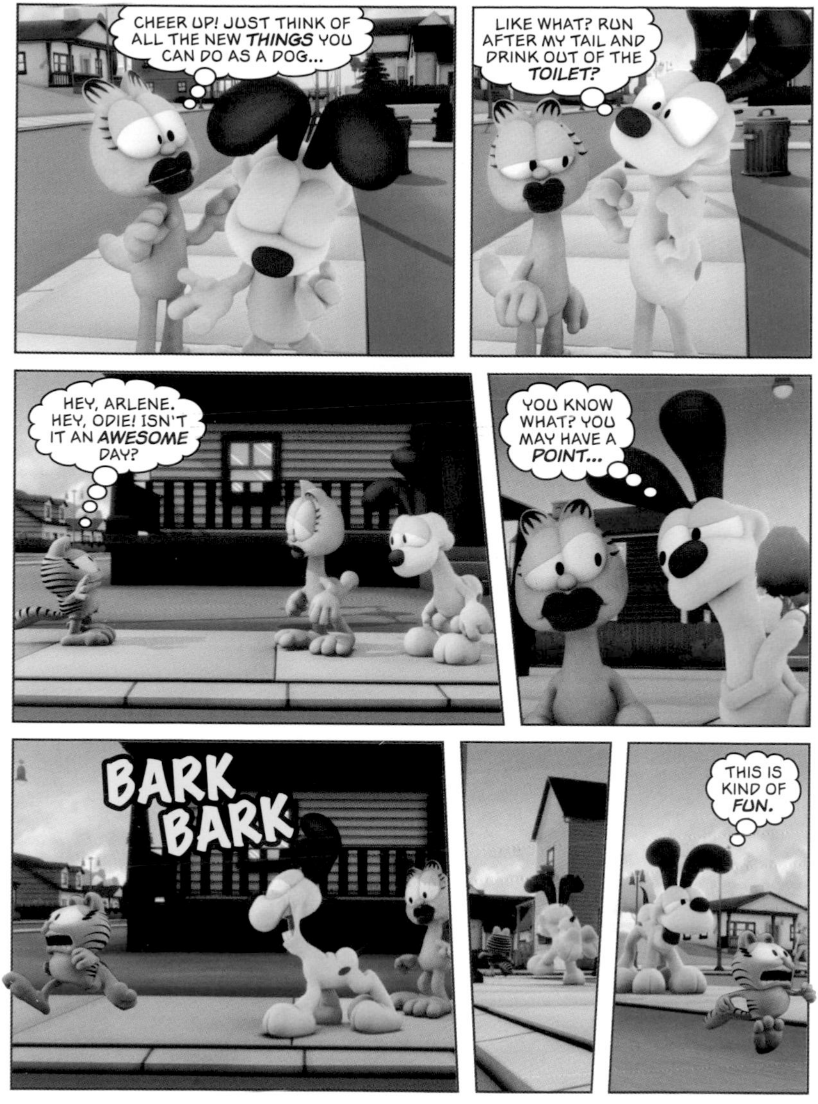
CHEER UP! JUST THINK OF ALL THE NEW THINGS YOU CAN DO AS A DOG...
LIKE WHAT? RUN AFTER MY TAIL AND DRINK OUT OF THE TOILET?
HEY, ARLENE. HEY, ODIE! ISN'T IT AN AWESOME DAY?
YOU KNOW WHAT? YOU MAY HAVE A POINT...
BARK
BARK
THIS IS KIND OF FUN.

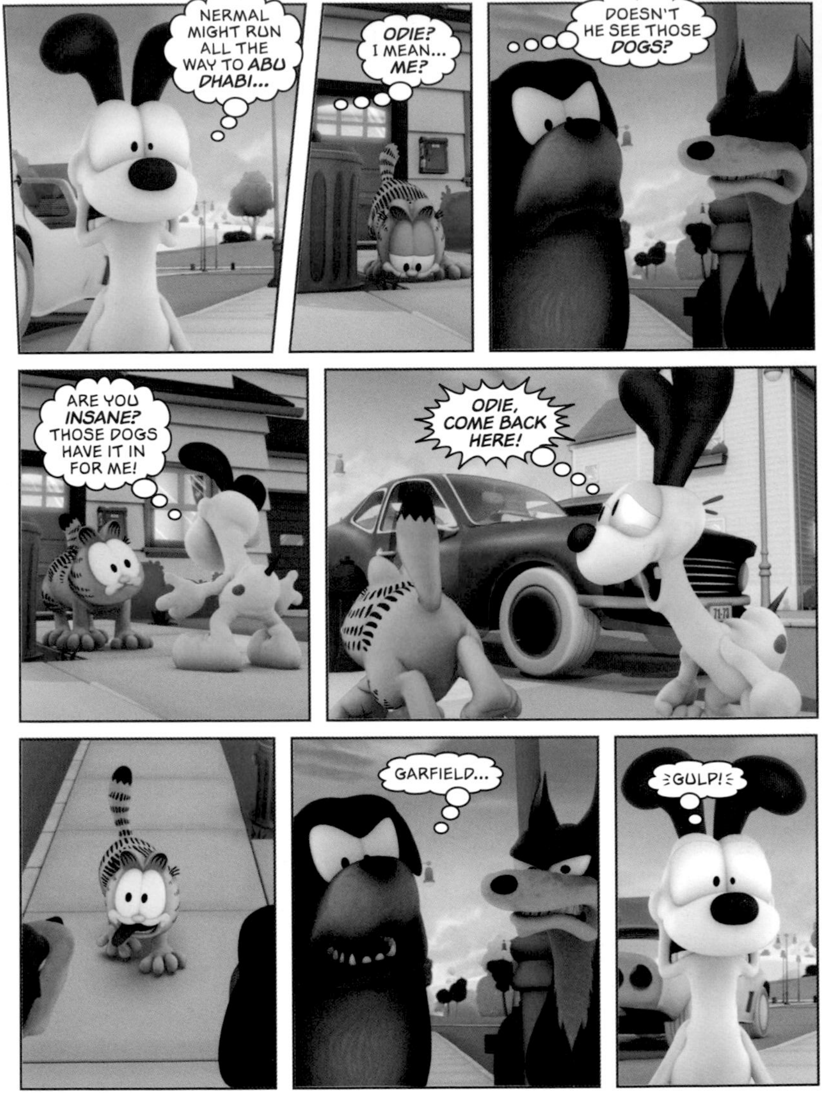
NERMAL MIGHT RUN ALL THE WAY TO ABU DHABI...
ODIE? I MEAN... ME?
DOESN'T HE SEE THOSE DOGS?
ARE YOU INSANE? THOSE DOGS HAVE IT IN FOR ME!
ODIE, COME BACK HERE!
GARFIELD...
GULP!

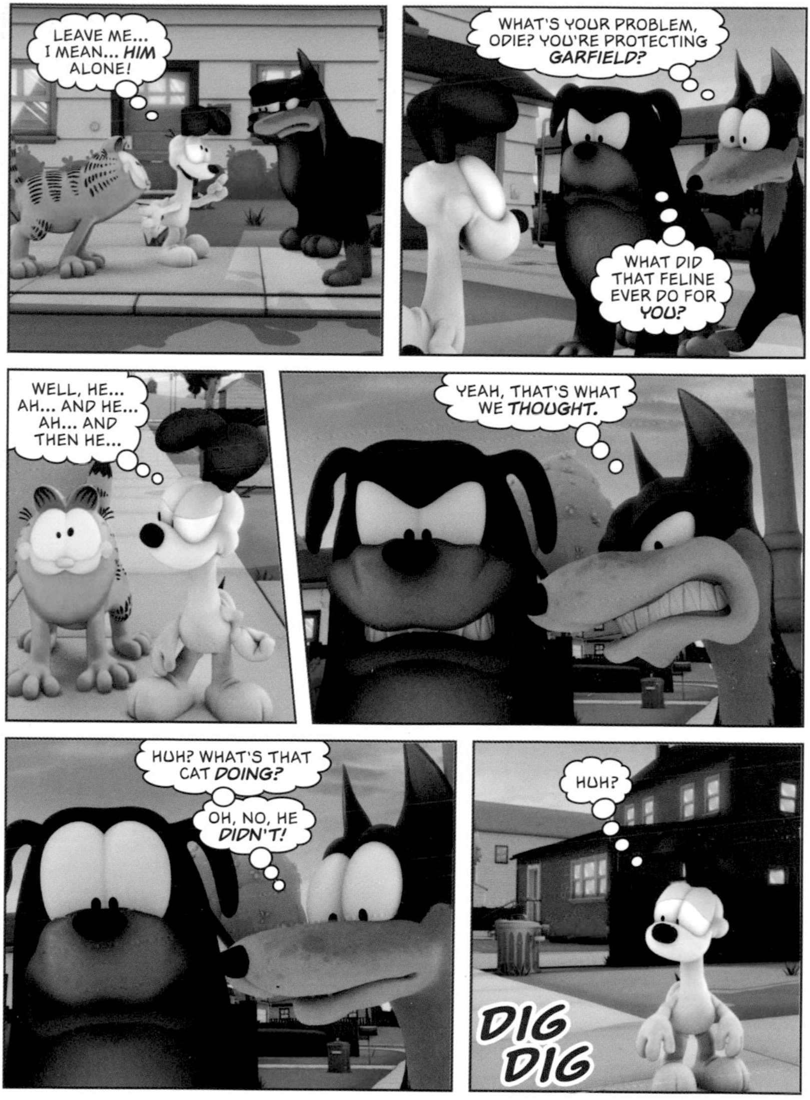
LEAVE ME... I MEAN... HIM ALONE!
WHAT'S YOUR PROBLEM, ODIE? YOU'RE PROTECTING GARFIELD?
WHAT DID THAT FELINE EVER DO FOR YOU?
WELL, HE... AH... AND HE... AH... AND THEN HE...
YEAH, THAT'S WHAT WE THOUGHT.
HUH? WHAT'S THAT CAT DOING?
OH, NO, HE DIDN'T!
HUH?
DIG DIG

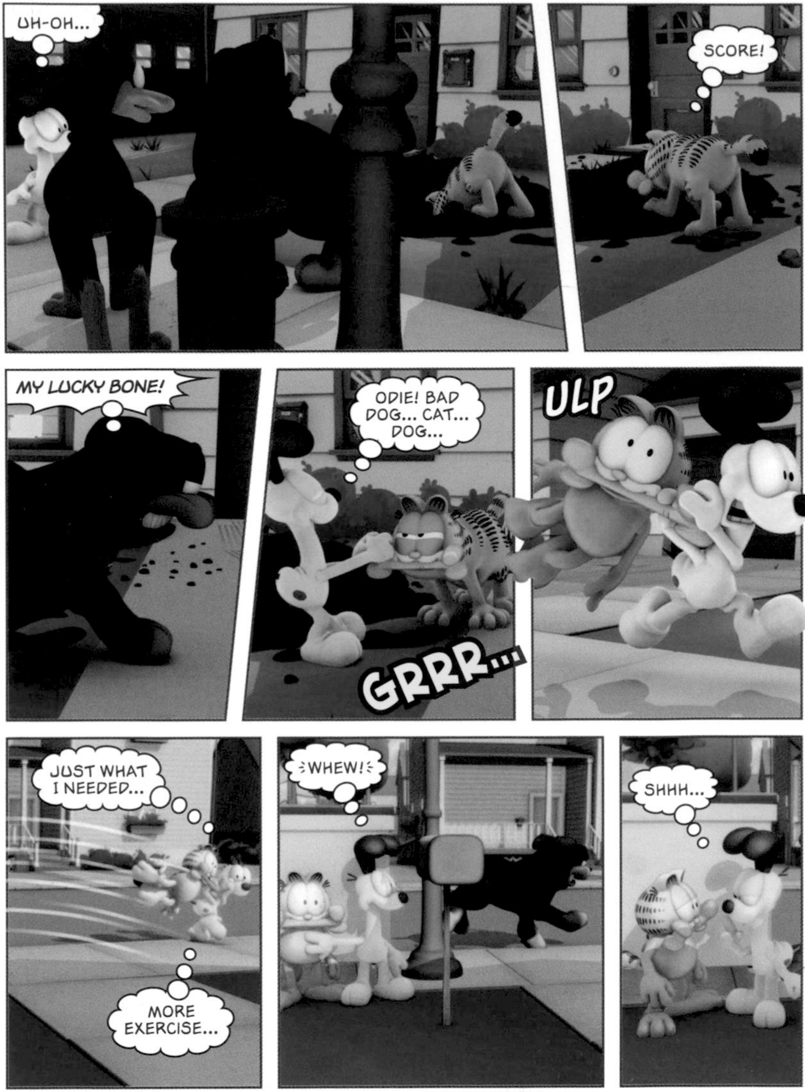
UH-OH...
SCORE!
MY LUCKY BONE!
ODIE! BAD DOG... CAT... DOG...
GRRR...
ULP
JUST WHAT I NEEDED...
MORE EXERCISE...
WHEW!
SHHH...

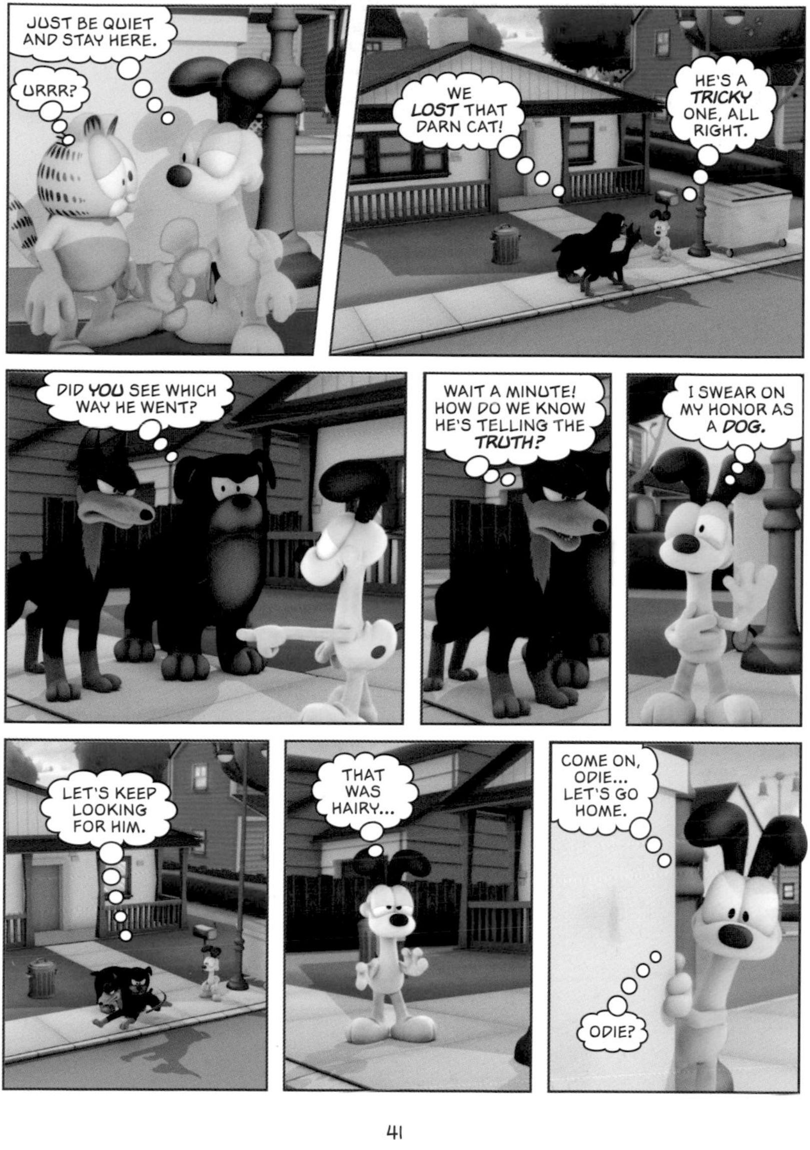
JUST BE QUIET AND STAY HERE.
URRR?
WE LOST THAT DARN CAT!
HE'S A TRICKY ONE, ALL RIGHT.
DID YOU SEE WHICH WAY HE WENT?
WAIT A MINUTE! HOW DO WE KNOW HE'S TELLING THE TRUTH?
I SWEAR ON MY HONOR AS A DOG.
LET'S KEEP LOOKING FOR HIM.
THAT WAS HAIRY...
COME ON, ODIE... LET'S GO HOME.
ODIE?

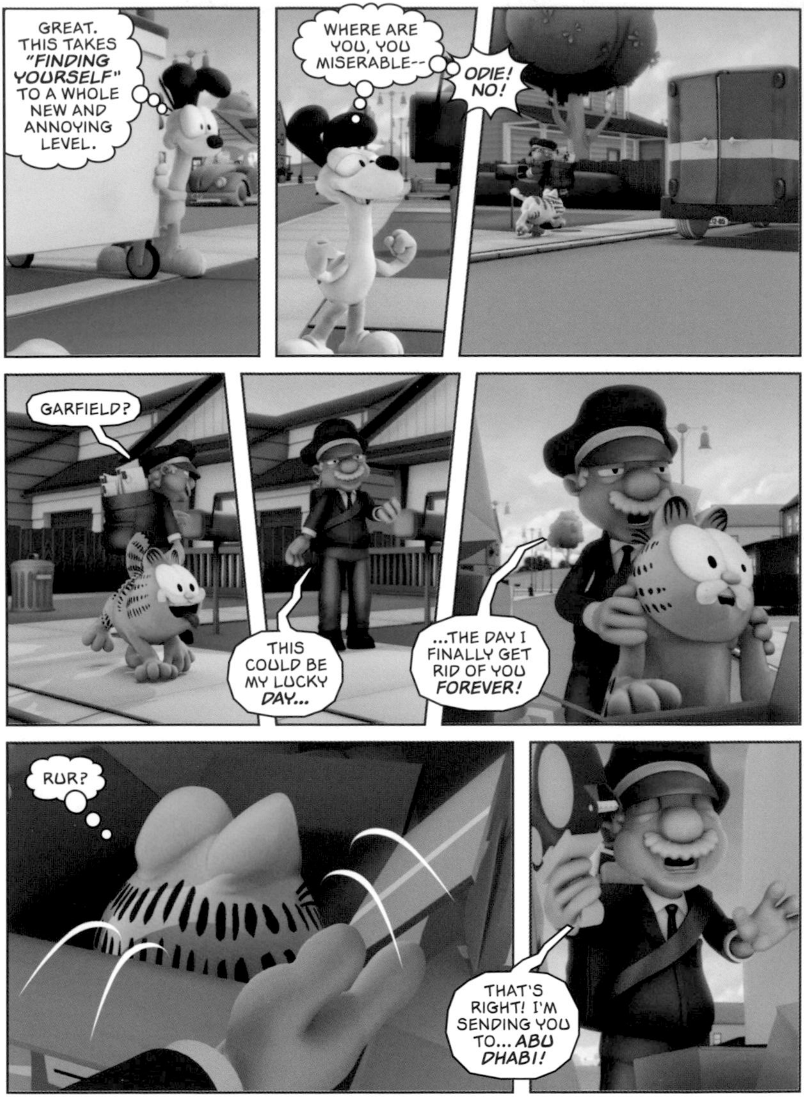
GREAT. THIS TAKES "FINDING YOURSELF" TO A WHOLE NEW AND ANNOYING LEVEL.
WHERE ARE YOU, YOU MISERABLE--
ODIE! NO!
GARFIELD?
THIS COULD BE MY LUCKY DAY...
...THE DAY I FINALLY GET RID OF YOU FOREVER!
RUR?
THAT'S RIGHT! I'M SENDING YOU TO... ABU DHABI!

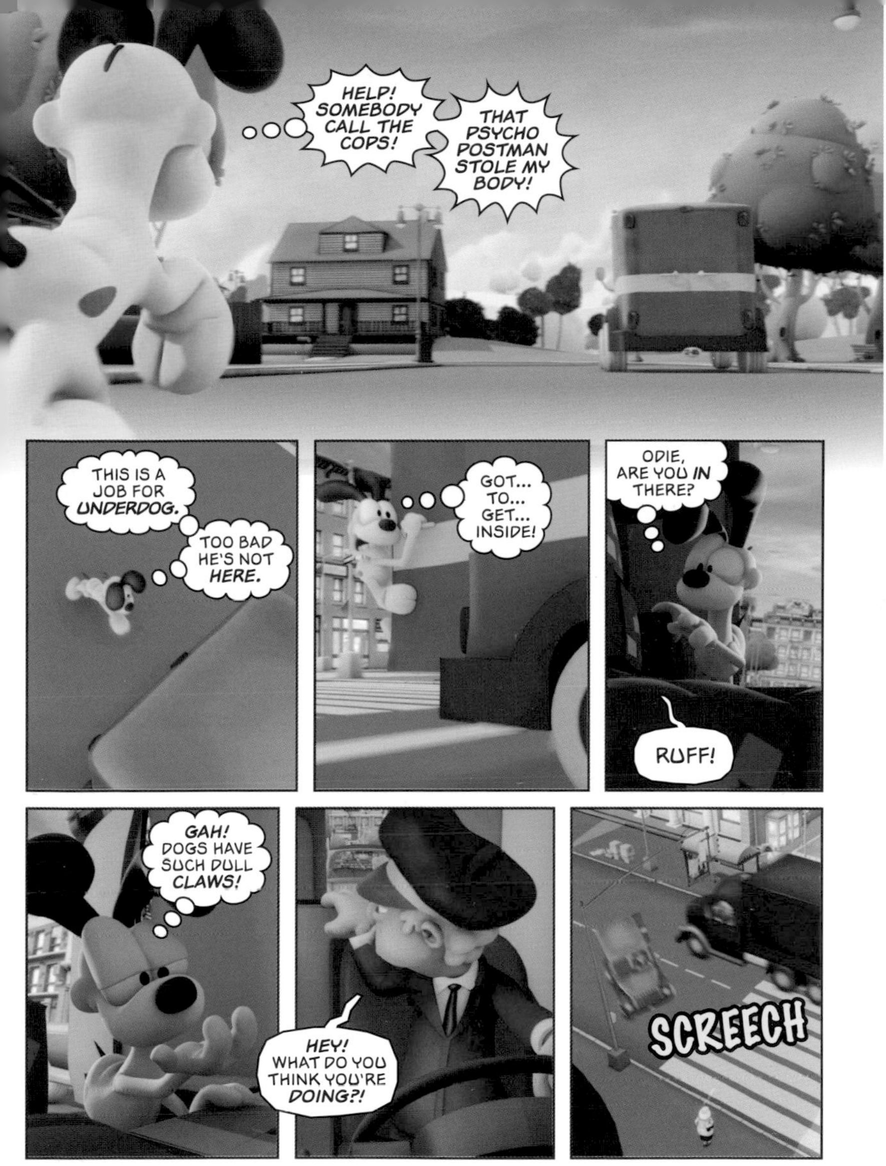
HELP! SOMEBODY CALL THE COPS!
THAT PSYCHO POSTMAN STOLE MY BODY!
THIS IS A JOB FOR UNDERDOG.
TOO BAD HE'S NOT HERE.
GOT... TO... GET... INSIDE!
ODIE, ARE YOU IN THERE?
RUFF!
GAH! DOGS HAVE SUCH DULL CLAWS!
HEY! WHAT DO YOU THINK YOU'RE DOING?!
SCREECH

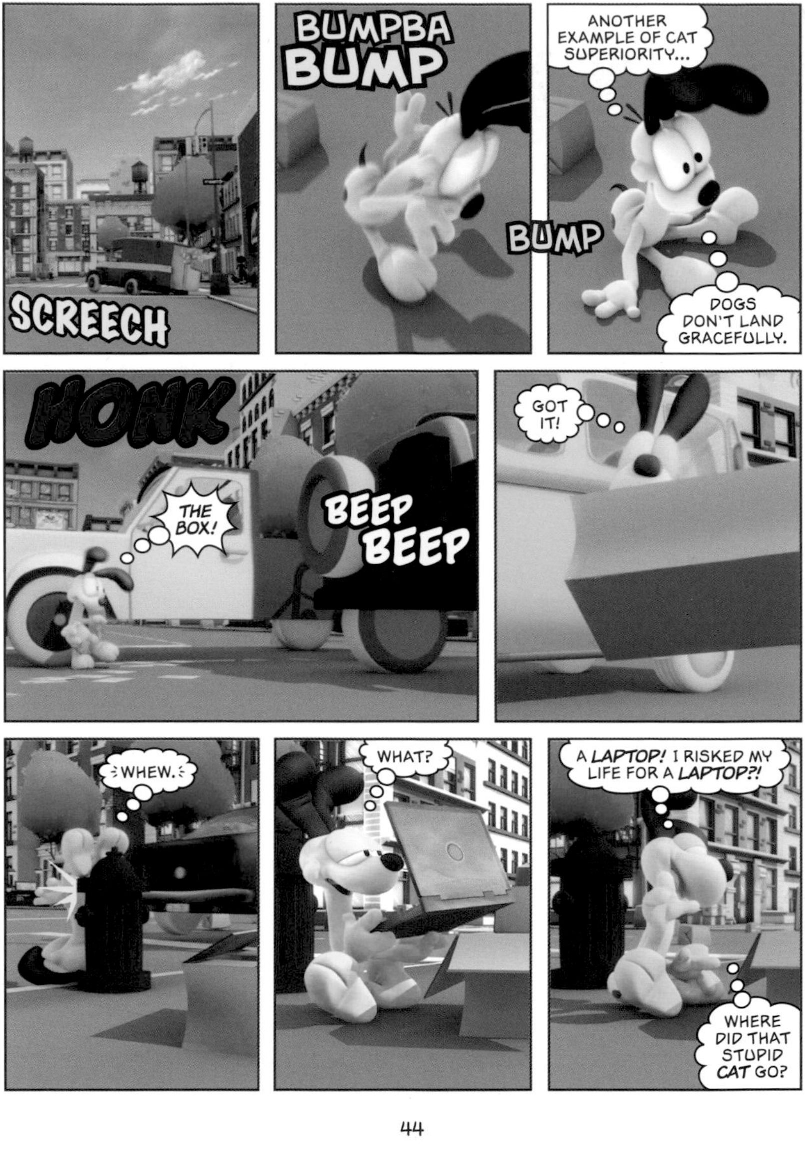
SCREECH
BUMPBA BUMP
BUMP
ANOTHER EXAMPLE OF CAT SUPERIORITY...
DOGS DON'T LAND GRACEFULLY.
HONK
THE BOX!
BEEP BEEP
GOT IT!
WHEW.
WHAT?
A LAPTOP! I RISKED MY LIFE FOR A LAPTOP?!
WHERE DID THAT STUPID CAT GO?

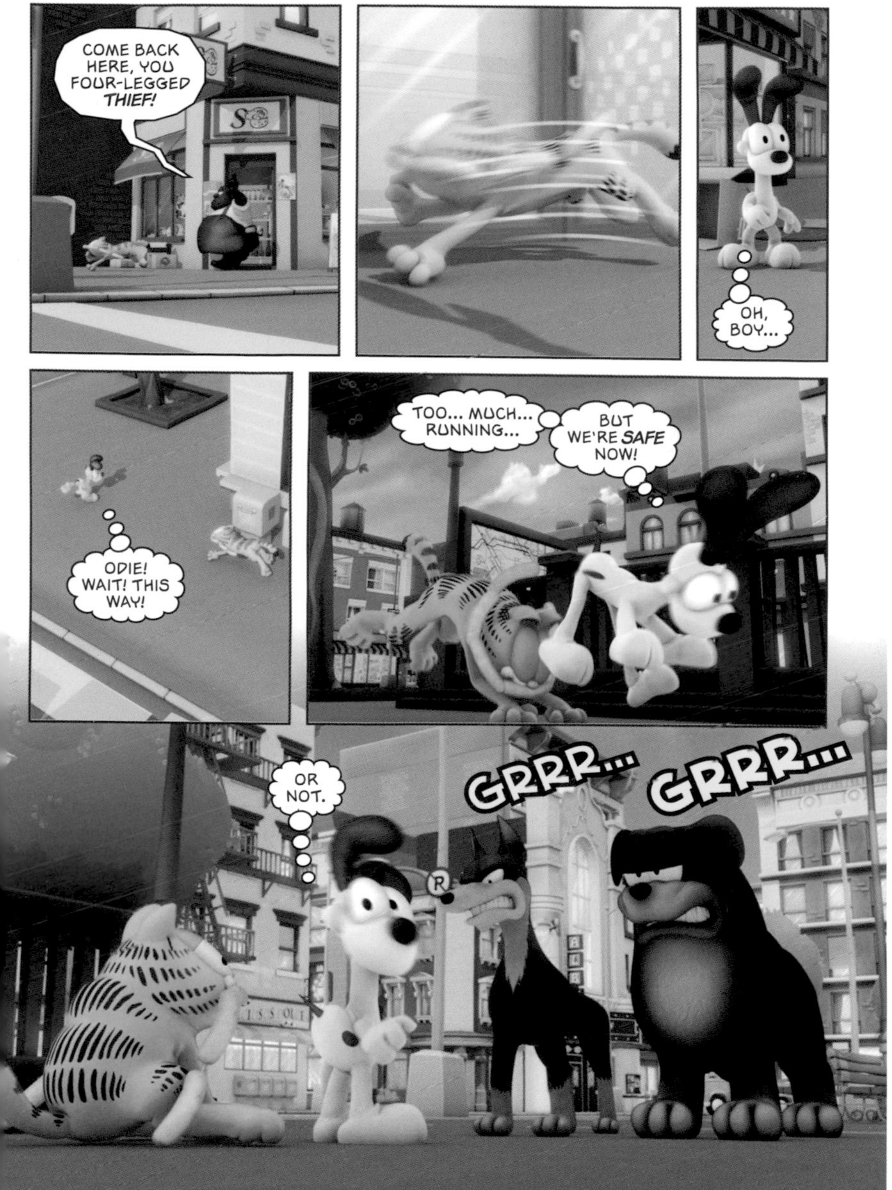
COME BACK HERE, YOU FOUR-LEGGED THIEF!
OH, BOY...
ODIE! WAIT! THIS WAY!
TOO... MUCH... RUNNING...
BUT WE'RE SAFE NOW!
OR NOT.
GRRR...
GRRR...

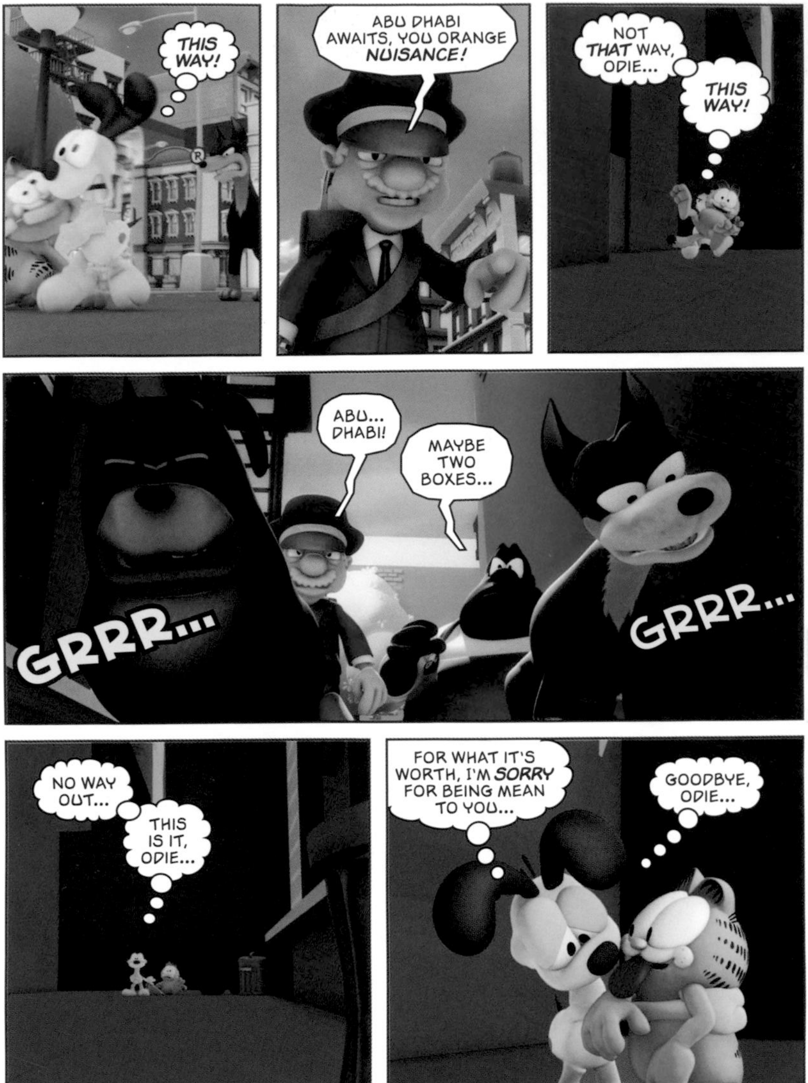
THIS WAY!
ABU DHABI AWAITS, YOU ORANGE NUISANCE!
NOT THAT WAY, ODIE...
THIS WAY!
ABU... DHABI!
MAYBE TWO BOXES...
GRRR...
GRRR...
NO WAY OUT...
THIS IS IT, ODIE...
FOR WHAT IT'S WORTH, I'M SORRY FOR BEING MEAN TO YOU...
GOODBYE, ODIE...

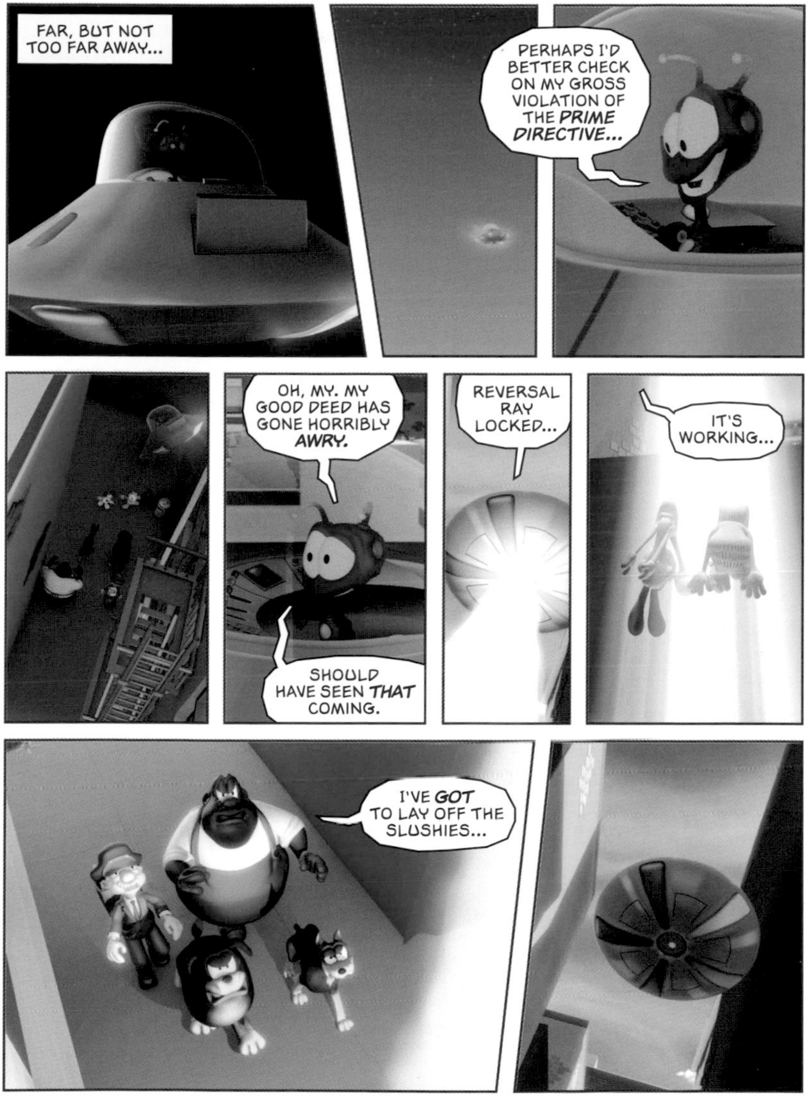
FAR, BUT NOT TOO FAR AWAY...
PERHAPS I'D BETTER CHECK ON MY GROSS VIOLATION OF THE PRIME DIRECTIVE...
OH, MY. MY GOOD DEED HAS GONE HORRIBLY AWRY.
SHOULD HAVE SEEN THAT COMING.
REVERSAL RAY LOCKED...
IT'S WORKING...
I'VE GOT TO LAY OFF THE SLUSHIES...

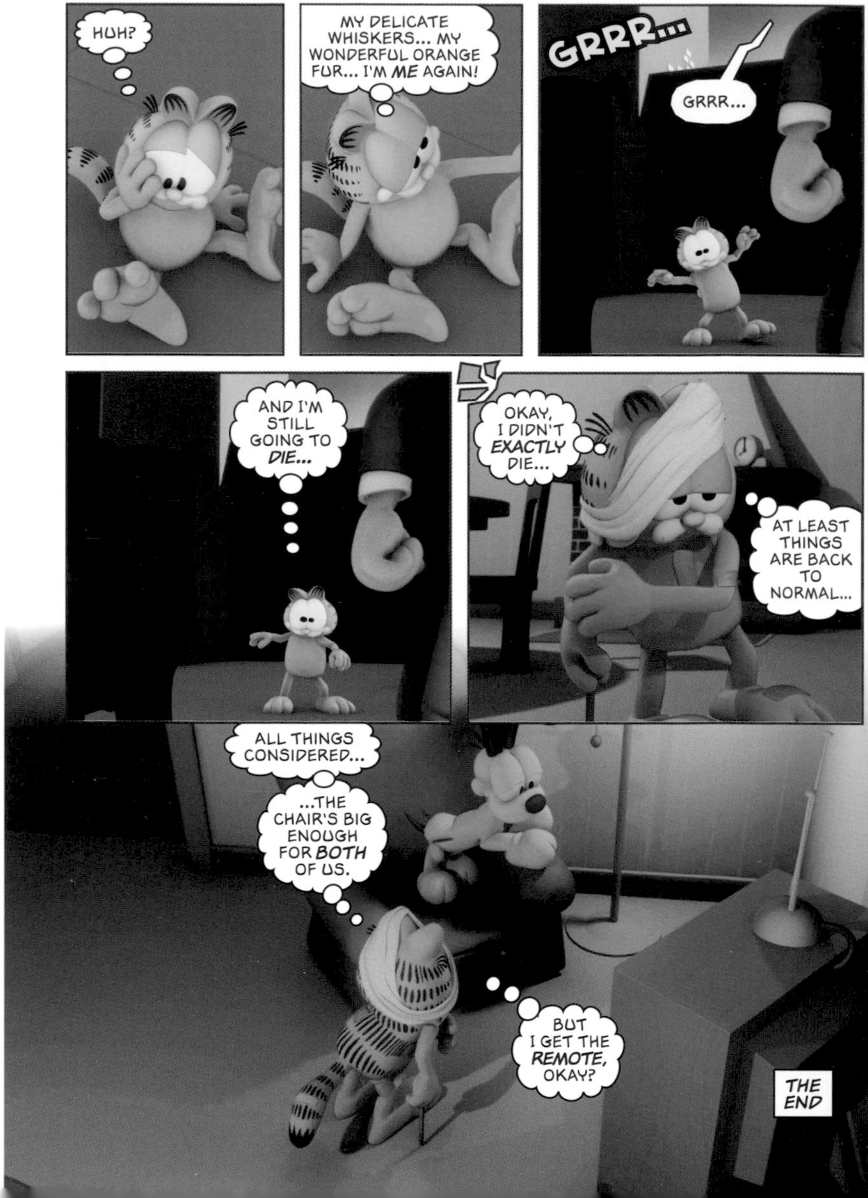

HUH?
MY DELICATE WHISKERS... MY WONDERFUL ORANGE FUR... I'M ME AGAIN!
GRRR...
GRRR...
AND I'M STILL GOING TO DIE...
OKAY, I DIDN'T EXACTLY DIE...
AT LEAST THINGS ARE BACK TO NORMAL...
ALL THINGS CONSIDERED...
...THE CHAIR'S BIG ENOUGH FOR BOTH OF US.
BUT I GET THE REMOTE, OKAY?
THE END

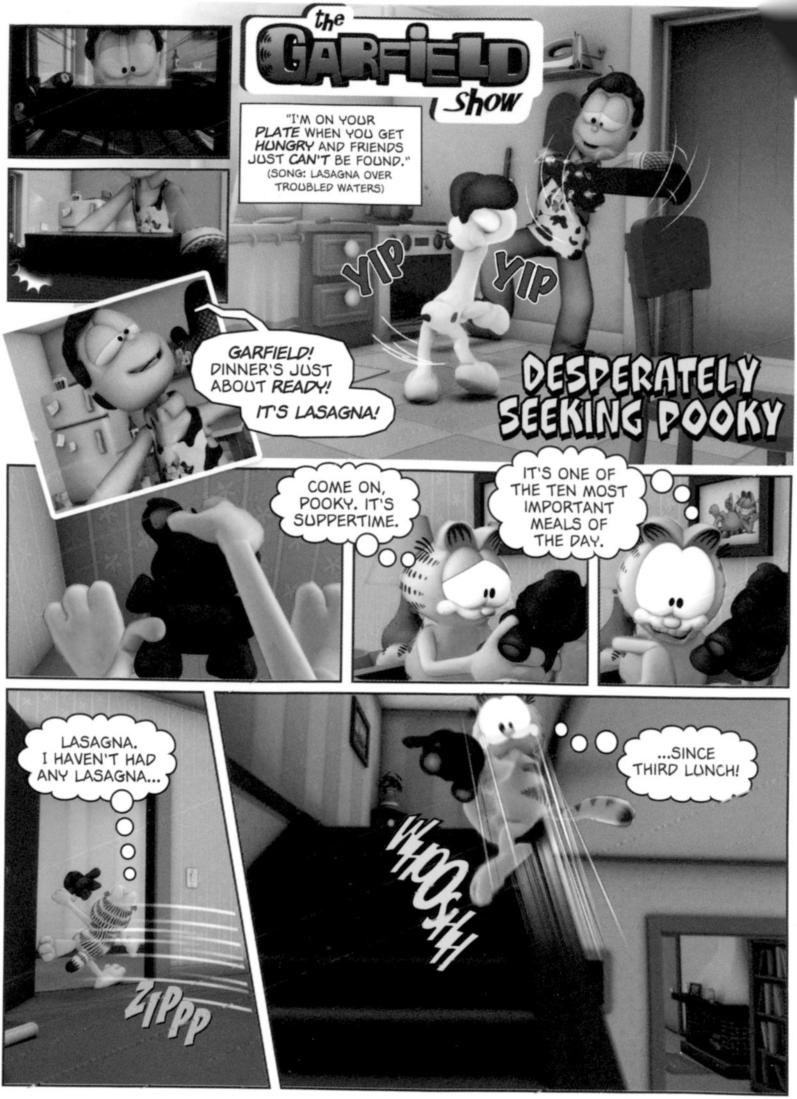

the GARFIELD show
"I'M ON YOUR PLATE WHEN YOU GET HUNGRY AND FRIENDS JUST CAN'T BE FOUND." (SONG: LASAGNA OVER TROUBLED WATERS)
YIP YIP
GARFIELD! DINNER'S JUST ABOUT READY!
IT'S LASAGNA!
DESPERATELY SEEKING POOKY
COME ON, POOKY. IT'S SUPPERTIME.
IT'S ONE OF THE TEN MOST IMPORTANT MEALS OF THE DAY.
LASAGNA. I HAVEN'T HAD ANY LASAGNA...
...SINCE THIRD LUNCH!
WHOOSH
ZIPPP

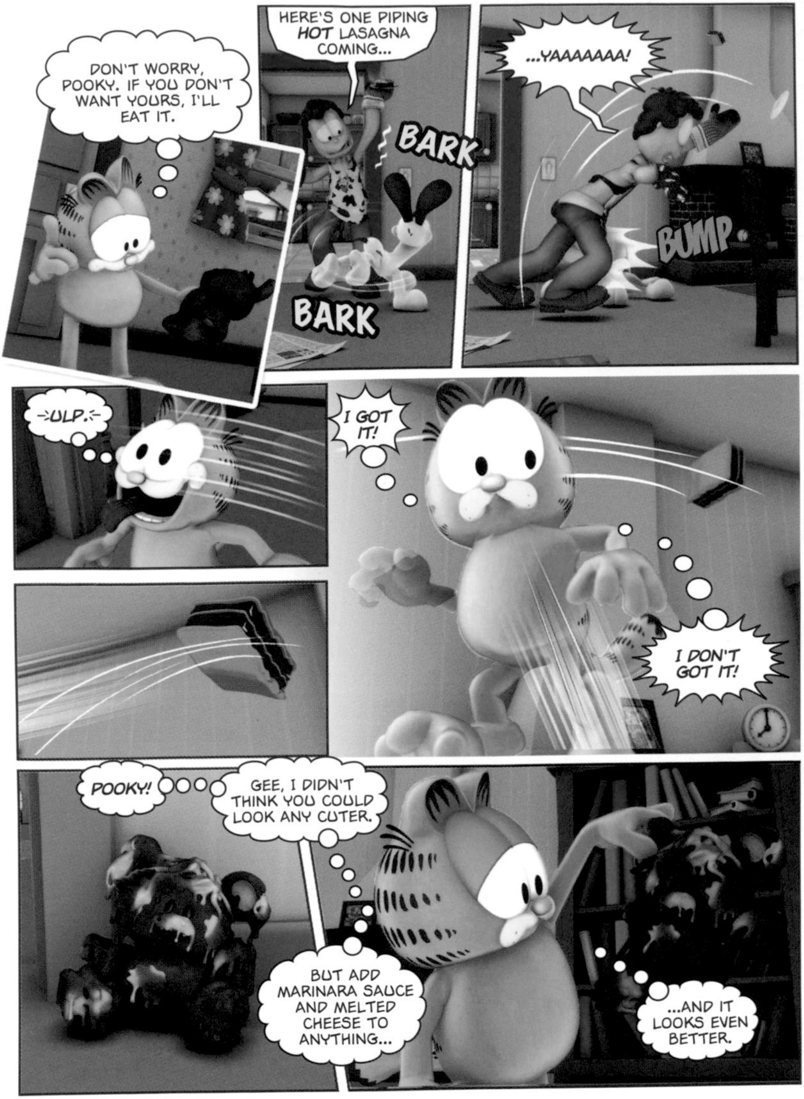
DON'T WORRY, POOKY. IF YOU DON'T WANT YOURS, I'LL EAT IT.
HERE'S ONE PIPING HOT LASAGNA COMING...
BARK
BARK
...YAAAAAAA!
BUMP
ULP.
I GOT IT!
I DON'T GOT IT!
POOKY!
GEE, I DIDN'T THINK YOU COULD LOOK ANY CUTER.
BUT ADD MARINARA SAUCE AND MELTED CHEESE TO ANYTHING...
...AND IT LOOKS EVEN BETTER.

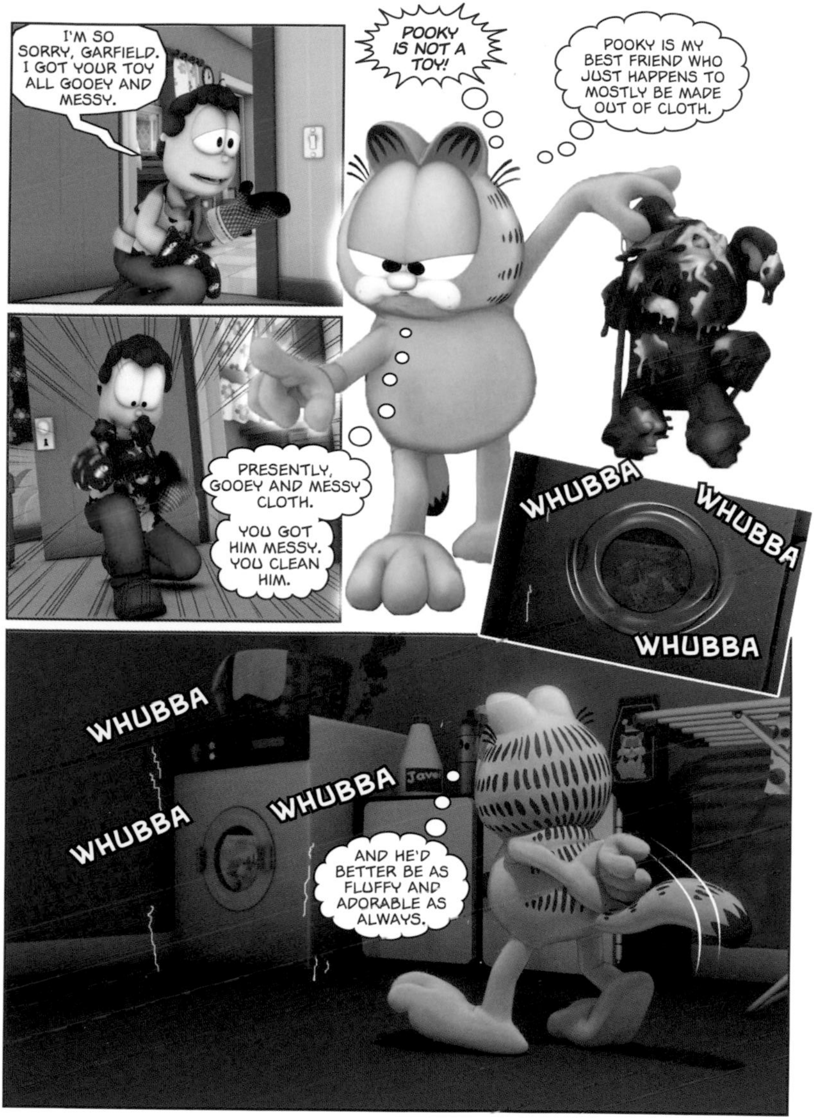
I'M SO SORRY, GARFIELD. I GOT YOUR TOY ALL GOOEY AND MESSY.
POOKY IS NOT A TOY!
POOKY IS MY BEST FRIEND WHO JUST HAPPENS TO MOSTLY BE MADE OUT OF CLOTH.
PRESENTLY, GOOEY AND MESSY CLOTH.
YOU GOT HIM MESSY. YOU CLEAN HIM.
WHUBBA
WHUBBA
WHUBBA
WHUBBA
WHUBBA
WHUBBA
AND HE'D BETTER BE AS FLUFFY AND ADORABLE AS ALWAYS.

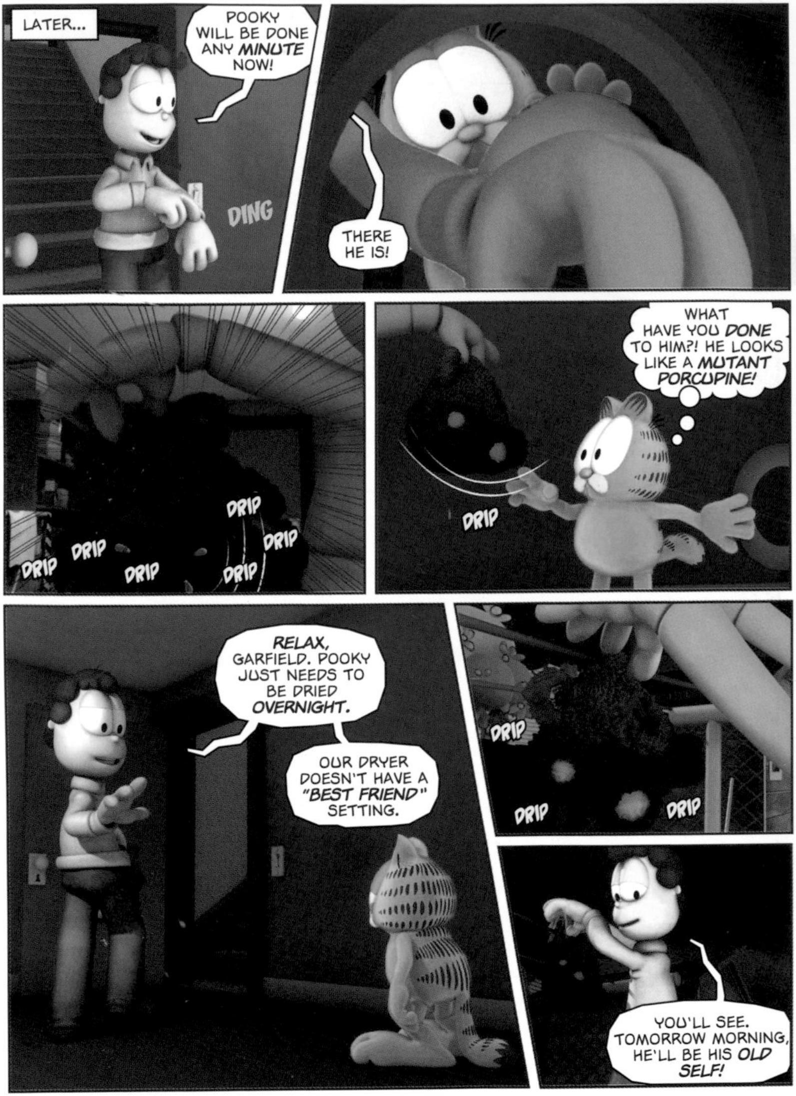

LATER...
POOKY WILL BE DONE ANY MINUTE NOW!
DING
THERE HE IS!
DRIP
DRIP
DRIP
DRIP
DRIP
DRIP
WHAT HAVE YOU DONE TO HIM?! HE LOOKS LIKE A MUTANT PORCUPINE!
DRIP
RELAX, GARFIELD. POOKY JUST NEEDS TO BE DRIED OVERNIGHT.
OUR DRYER DOESN'T HAVE A "BEST FRIEND" SETTING.
DRIP
DRIP
DRIP
YOU'LL SEE. TOMORROW MORNING, HE'LL BE HIS OLD SELF!

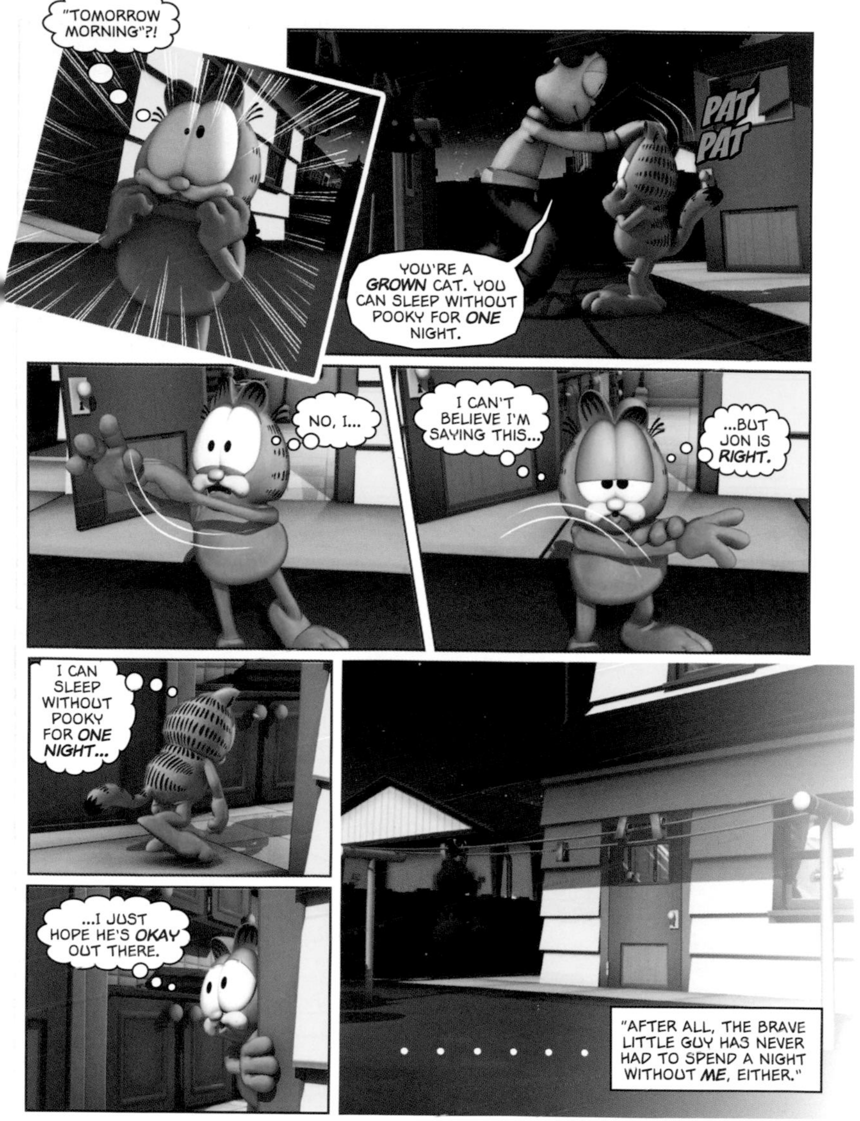
"TOMORROW MORNING"?!
PAT PAT
YOU'RE A GROWN CAT. YOU CAN SLEEP WITHOUT POOKY FOR ONE NIGHT.
NO, I...
I CAN'T BELIEVE I'M SAYING THIS...
...BUT JON IS RIGHT.
I CAN SLEEP WITHOUT POOKY FOR ONE NIGHT...
...I JUST HOPE HE'S OKAY OUT THERE.
"AFTER ALL, THE BRAVE LITTLE GUY HAS NEVER HAD TO SPEND A NIGHT WITHOUT ME, EITHER."

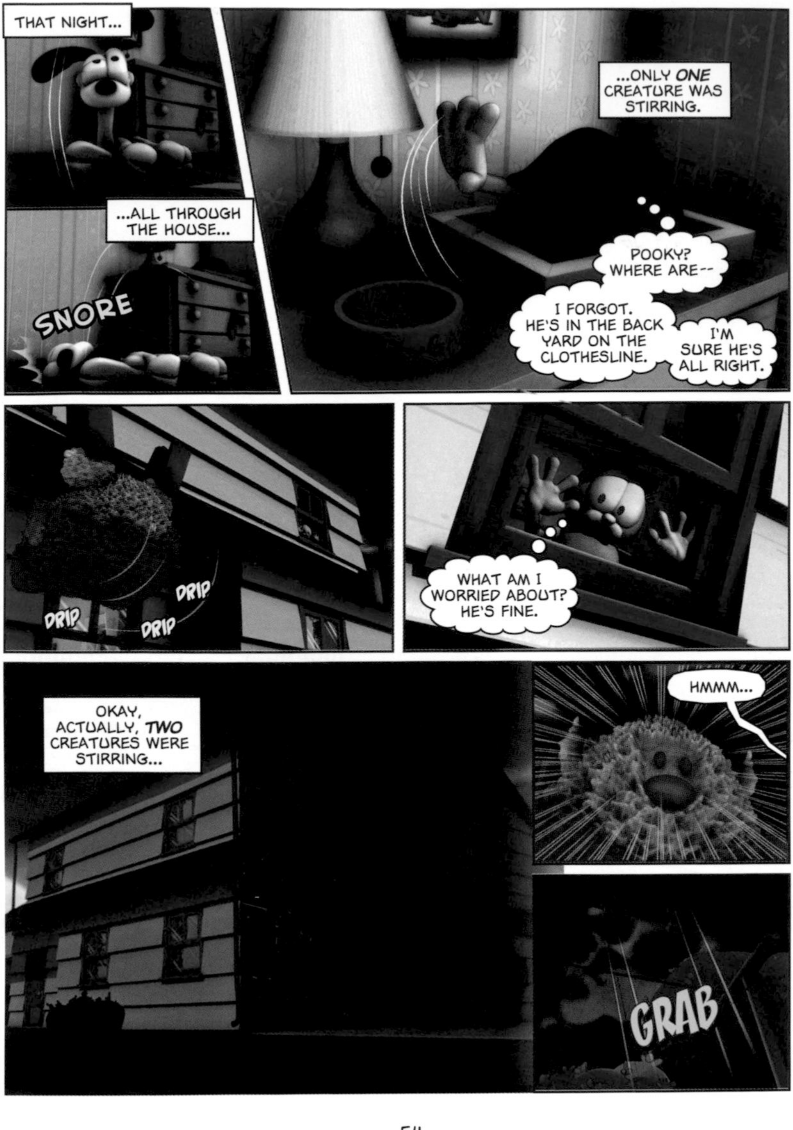
THAT NIGHT...
...ALL THROUGH THE HOUSE...
SNORE
...ONLY ONE CREATURE WAS STIRRING.
POOKY? WHERE ARE--
I FORGOT. HE'S IN THE BACK YARD ON THE CLOTHESLINE.
I'M SURE HE'S ALL RIGHT.
DRIP
DRIP
DRIP
WHAT AM I WORRIED ABOUT? HE'S FINE.
OKAY, ACTUALLY, TWO CREATURES WERE STIRRING...
HMMM...
GRAB

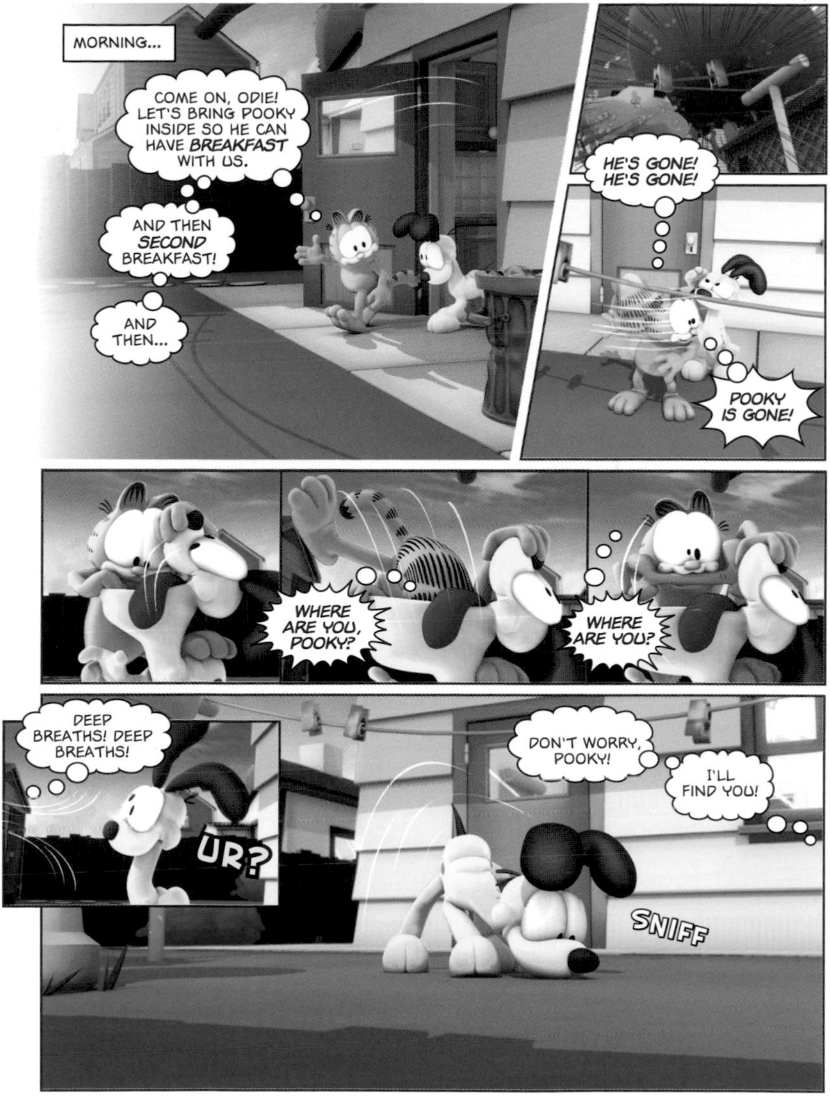
MORNING...
COME ON, ODIE! LET'S BRING POOKY INSIDE SO HE CAN HAVE BREAKFAST WITH US.
AND THEN SECOND BREAKFAST!
AND THEN...
HE'S GONE! HE'S GONE!
POOKY IS GONE!
WHERE ARE YOU, POOKY?
WHERE ARE YOU?
DEEP BREATHS! DEEP BREATHS!
UR?
DON'T WORRY, POOKY!
I'LL FIND YOU!
SNIFF

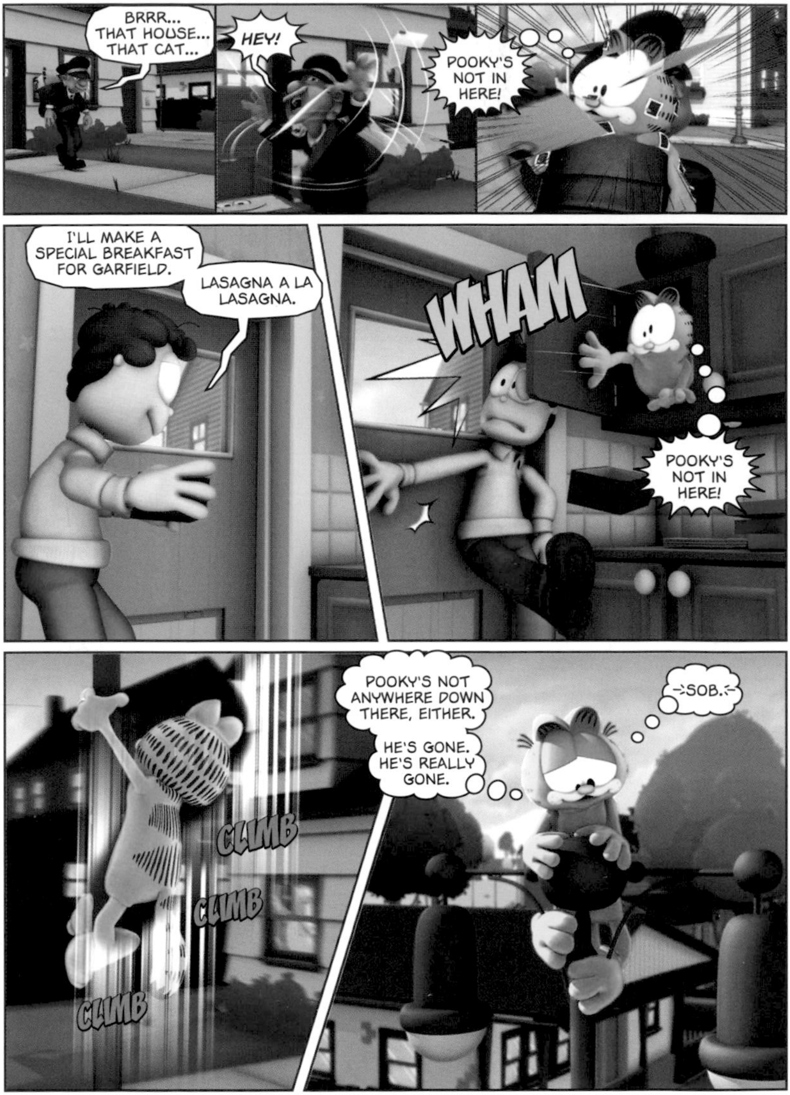
BRRR... THAT HOUSE... THAT CAT...
HEY!
POOKY'S NOT IN HERE!
I'LL MAKE A SPECIAL BREAKFAST FOR GARFIELD.
LASAGNA A LA LASAGNA.
WHAM
POOKY'S NOT IN HERE!
CLIMB
CLIMB
CLIMB
POOKY'S NOT ANYWHERE DOWN THERE, EITHER.
HE'S GONE. HE'S REALLY GONE.
SOB.

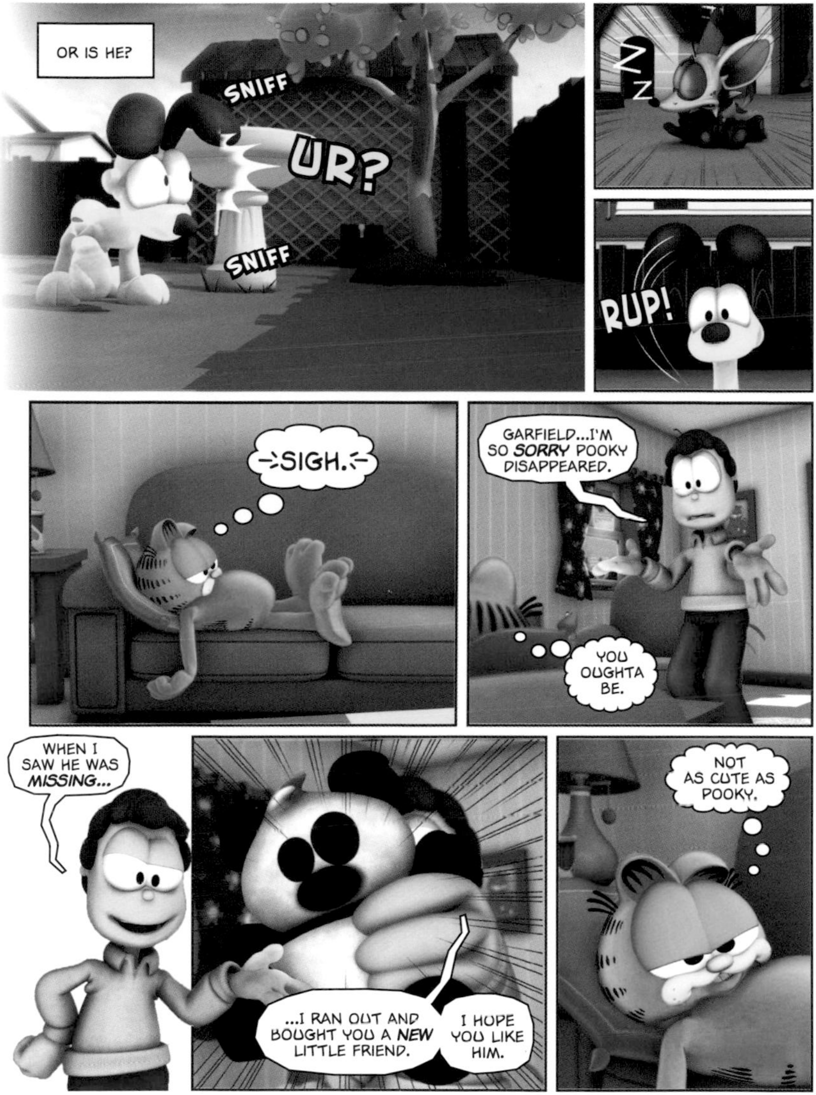
OR IS HE?
SNIFF
UR?
SNIFF
Z
Z
RUP!
-SIGH.-
GARFIELD...I'M SO SORRY POOKY DISAPPEARED.
YOU OUGHTA BE.
WHEN I SAW HE WAS MISSING...
...I RAN OUT AND BOUGHT YOU A NEW LITTLE FRIEND.
I HOPE YOU LIKE HIM.
NOT AS CUTE AS POOKY.

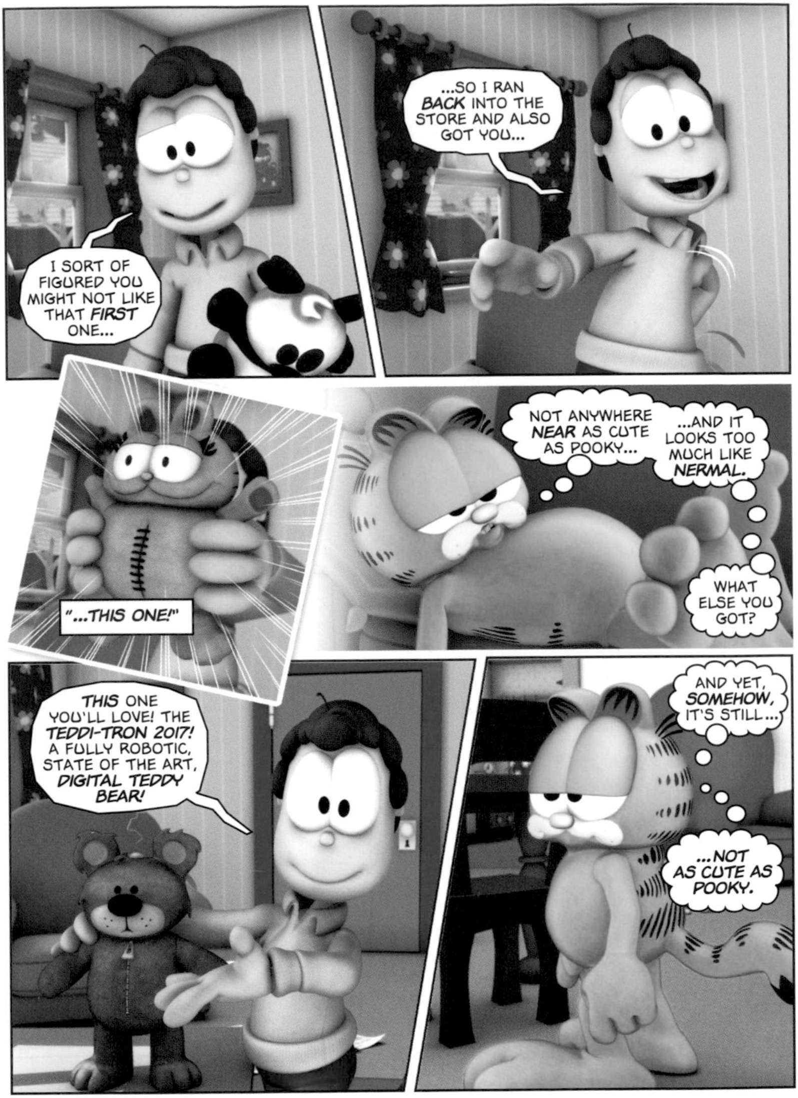
I SORT OF FIGURED YOU MIGHT NOT LIKE THAT FIRST ONE...
...SO I RAN BACK INTO THE STORE AND ALSO GOT YOU...
"...THIS ONE!"
NOT ANYWHERE NEAR AS CUTE AS POOKY...
...AND IT LOOKS TOO MUCH LIKE NERMAL.
WHAT ELSE YOU GOT?
THIS ONE YOU'LL LOVE! THE TEDDI-TRON 2017! A FULLY ROBOTIC, STATE OF THE ART, DIGITAL TEDDY BEAR!
AND YET, SOMEHOW, IT'S STILL...
...NOT AS CUTE AS POOKY.

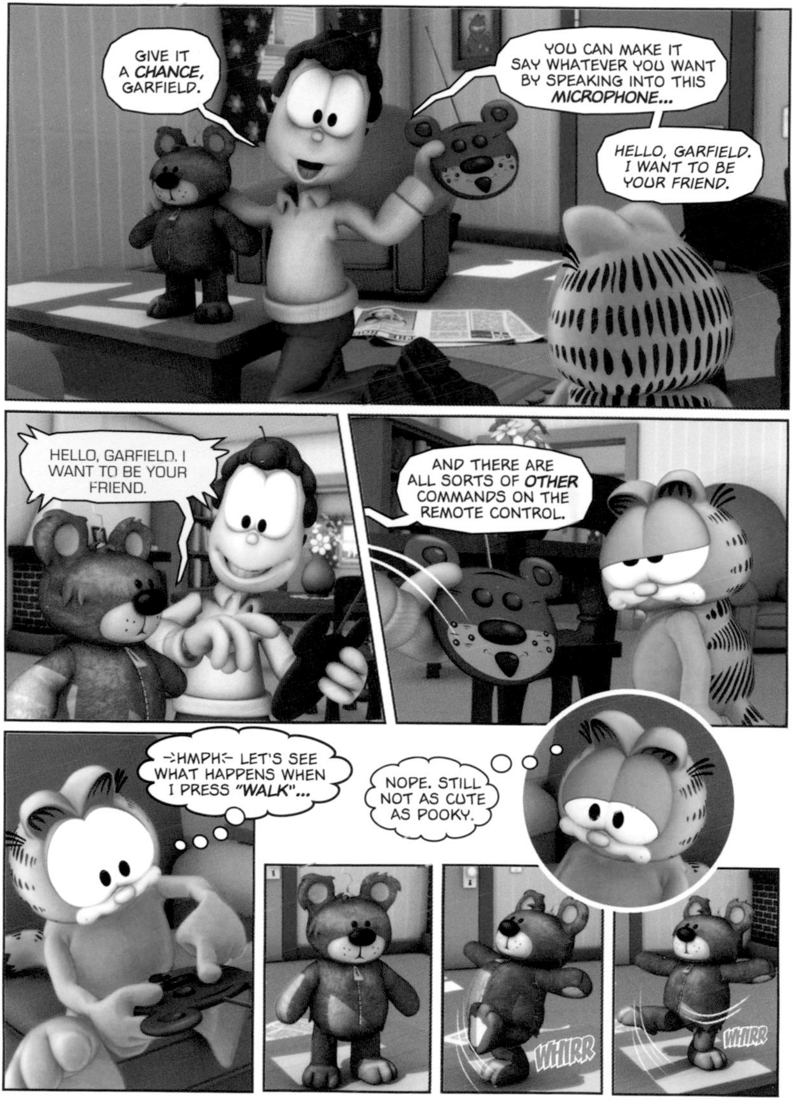
GIVE IT A CHANCE, GARFIELD.
YOU CAN MAKE IT SAY WHATEVER YOU WANT BY SPEAKING INTO THIS MICROPHONE...
HELLO, GARFIELD. I WANT TO BE YOUR FRIEND.
HELLO, GARFIELD. I WANT TO BE YOUR FRIEND.
AND THERE ARE ALL SORTS OF OTHER COMMANDS ON THE REMOTE CONTROL.
-HMPH- LET'S SEE WHAT HAPPENS WHEN I PRESS "WALK"...
NOPE. STILL NOT AS CUTE AS POOKY.
WHIRR
WHIRR

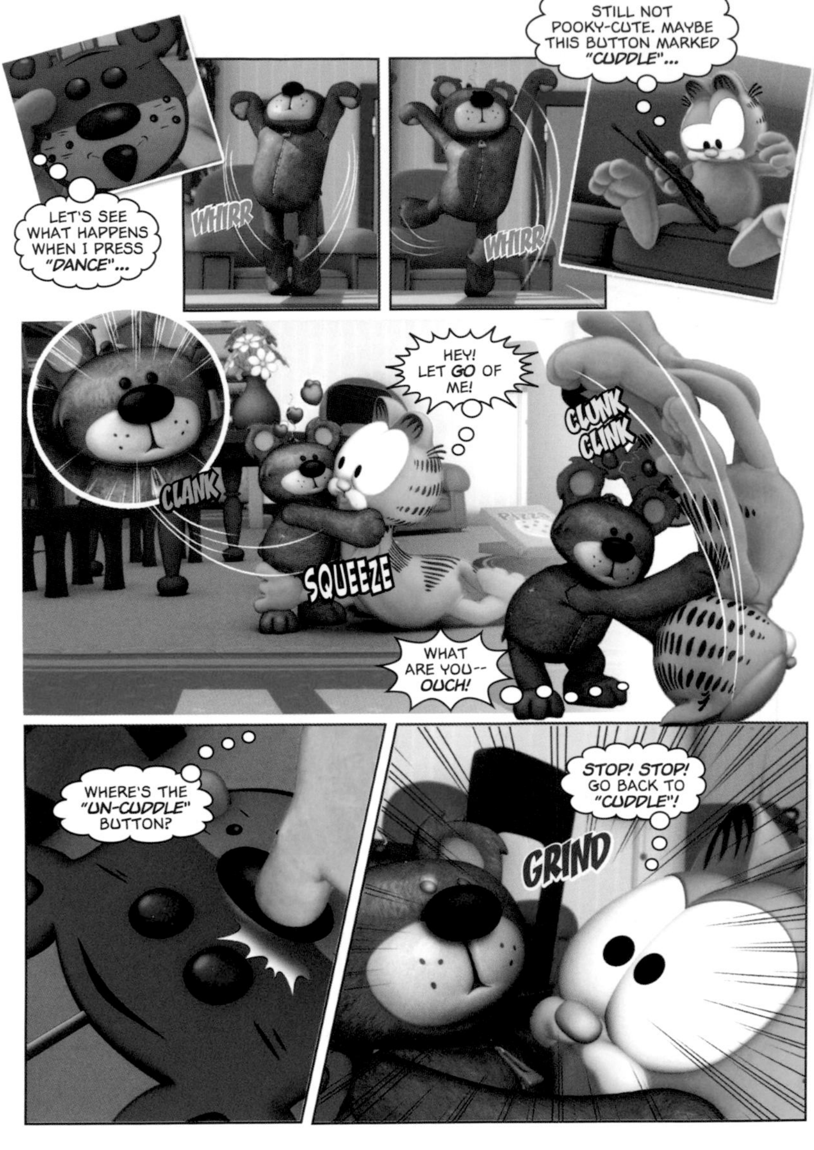
LET'S SEE WHAT HAPPENS WHEN I PRESS "DANCE"...
WHIRR
WHIRR
STILL NOT POOKY-CUTE. MAYBE THIS BUTTON MARKED "CUDDLE"...
CLANK
HEY! LET GO OF ME!
SQUEEZE
CLUNK CLINK
WHAT ARE YOU-- OUCH!
WHERE'S THE "UN-CUDDLE" BUTTON?
STOP! STOP! GO BACK TO "CUDDLE"!
GRIND

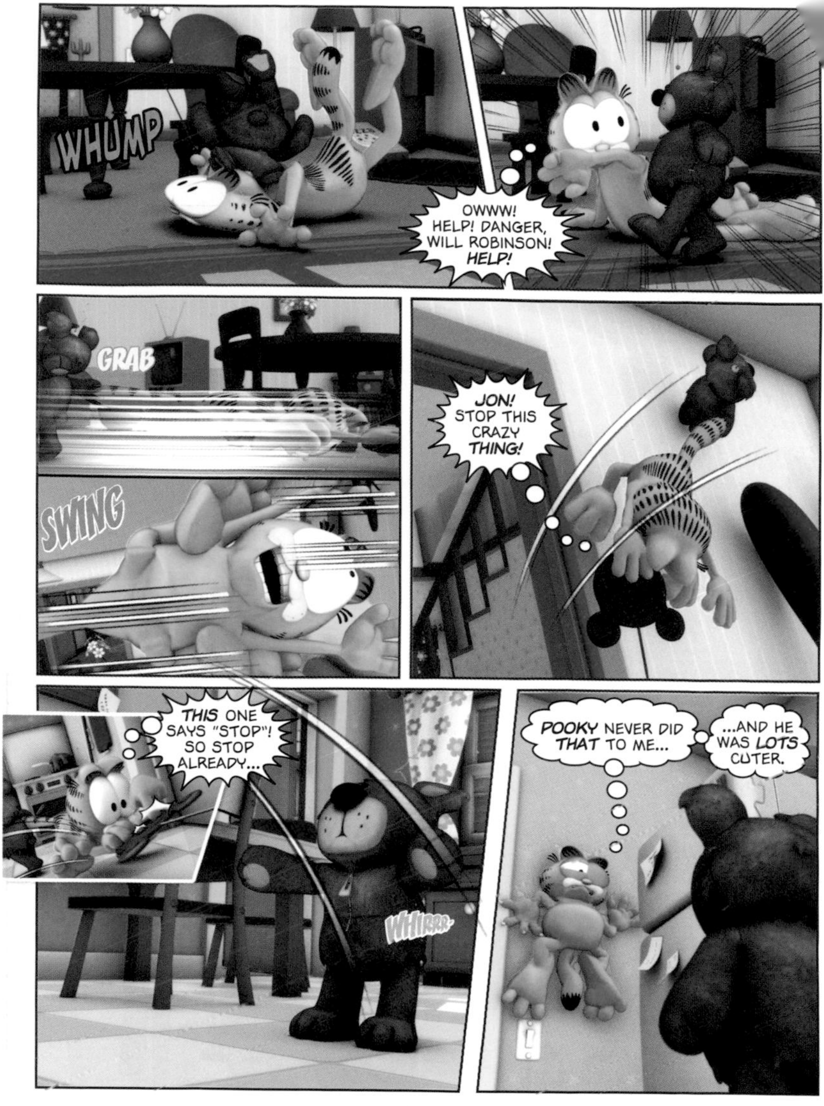

WHUMP
OWWW! HELP! DANGER, WILL ROBINSON! HELP!
GRAB
SWING
JON! STOP THIS CRAZY THING!
THIS ONE SAYS "STOP"! SO STOP ALREADY...
WHIRRR-
POOKY NEVER DID THAT TO ME...
...AND HE WAS LOTS CUTER.

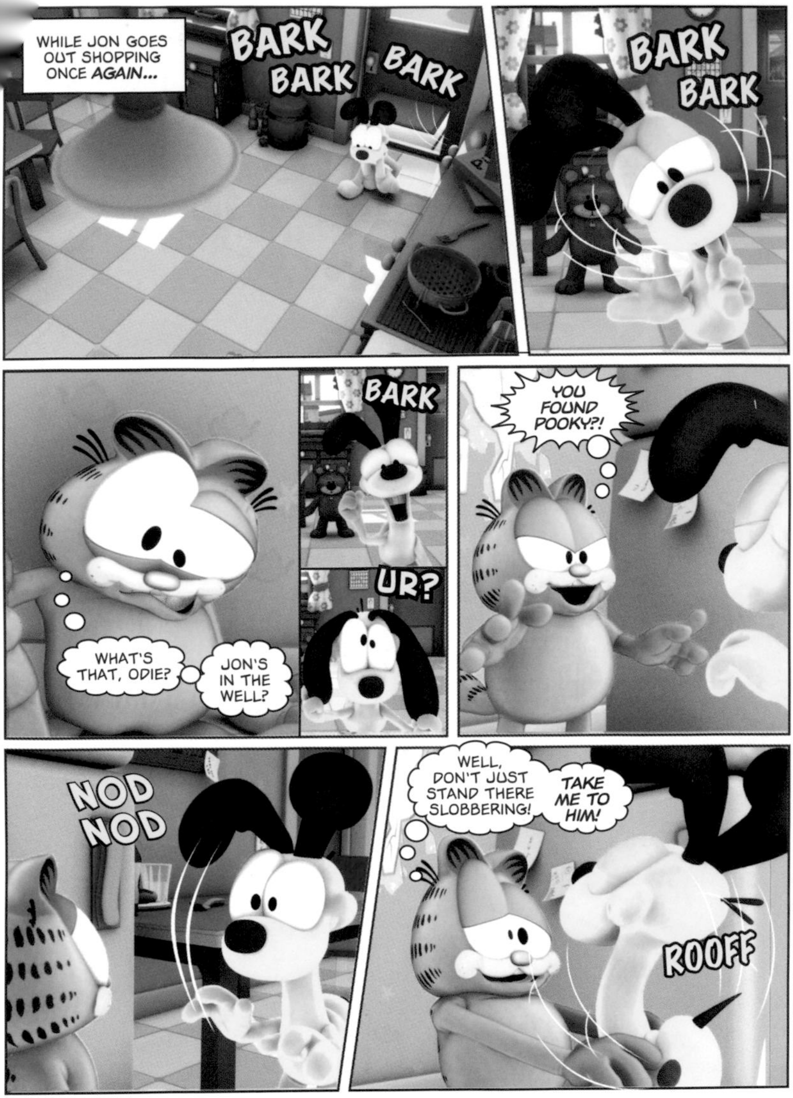
WHILE JON GOES OUT SHOPPING ONCE AGAIN...
BARK
BARK
BARK
BARK
BARK
BARK
WHAT'S THAT, ODIE?
JON'S IN THE WELL?
UR?
YOU FOUND POOKY?!
NOD NOD
WELL, DON'T JUST STAND THERE SLOBBERING!
TAKE ME TO HIM!
ROOFF

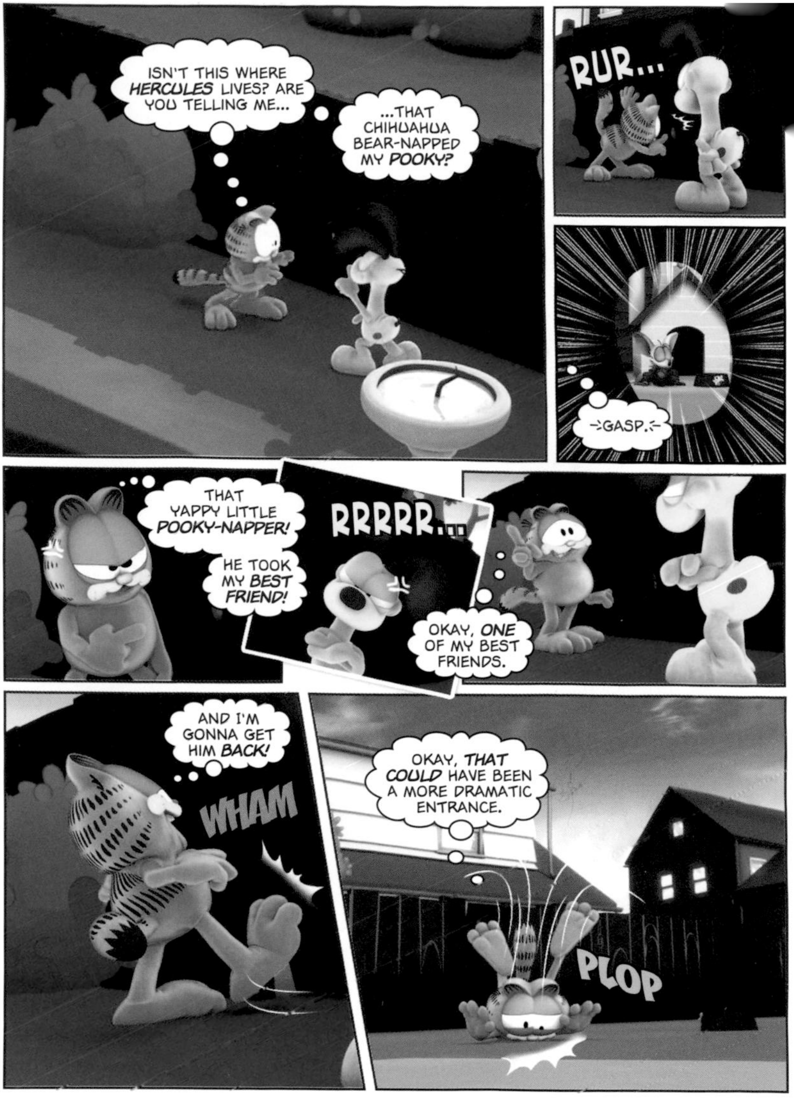

ISN'T THIS WHERE *HERCULES* LIVES? ARE YOU TELLING ME...
...THAT CHIHUAHUA BEAR-NAPPED MY *POOKY?*
RUR...
-GASP.-
THAT YAPPY LITTLE *POOKY-NAPPER!*
HE TOOK MY *BEST FRIEND!*
RRRRR...
OKAY, *ONE* OF MY BEST FRIENDS.
AND I'M GONNA GET HIM *BACK!*
WHAM
OKAY, *THAT COULD* HAVE BEEN A MORE DRAMATIC ENTRANCE.
PLOP

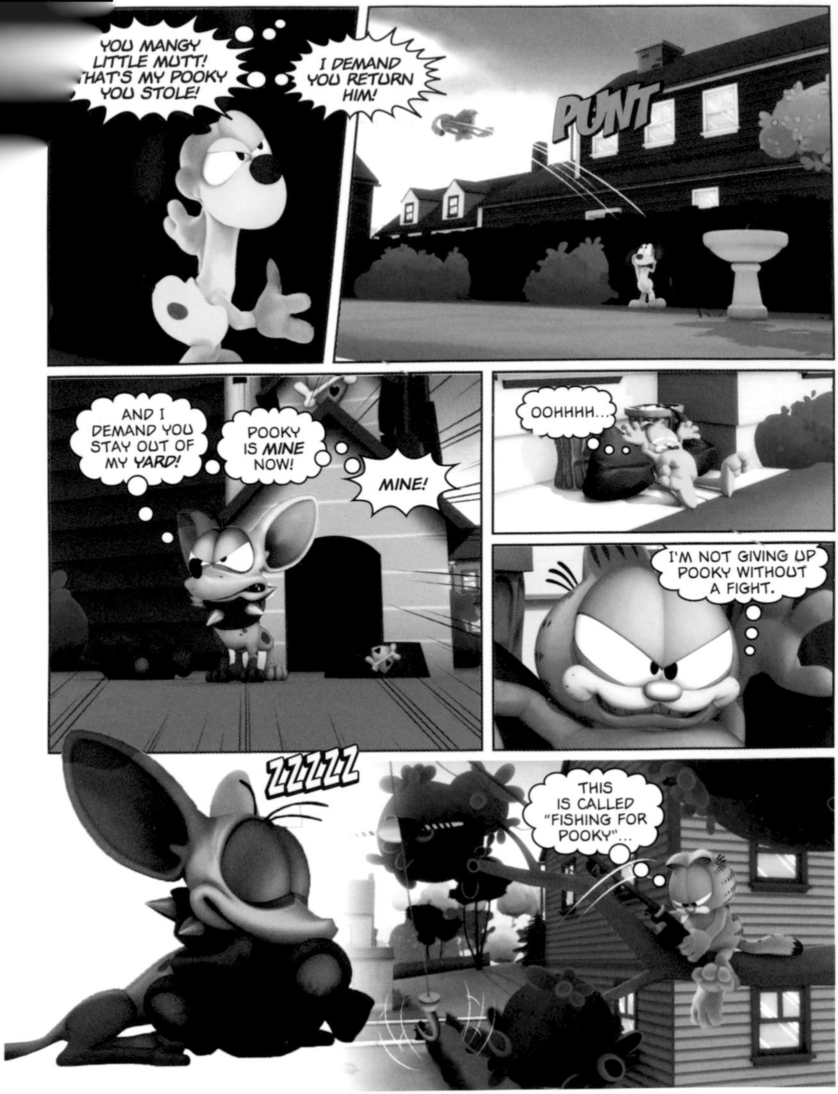
YOU MANGY LITTLE MUTT! THAT'S MY POOKY YOU STOLE!
I DEMAND YOU RETURN HIM!
PUNT
AND I DEMAND YOU STAY OUT OF MY YARD!
POOKY IS MINE NOW!
MINE!
OOHHHH...
I'M NOT GIVING UP POOKY WITHOUT A FIGHT.
ZZZZZ
THIS IS CALLED "FISHING FOR POOKY"...

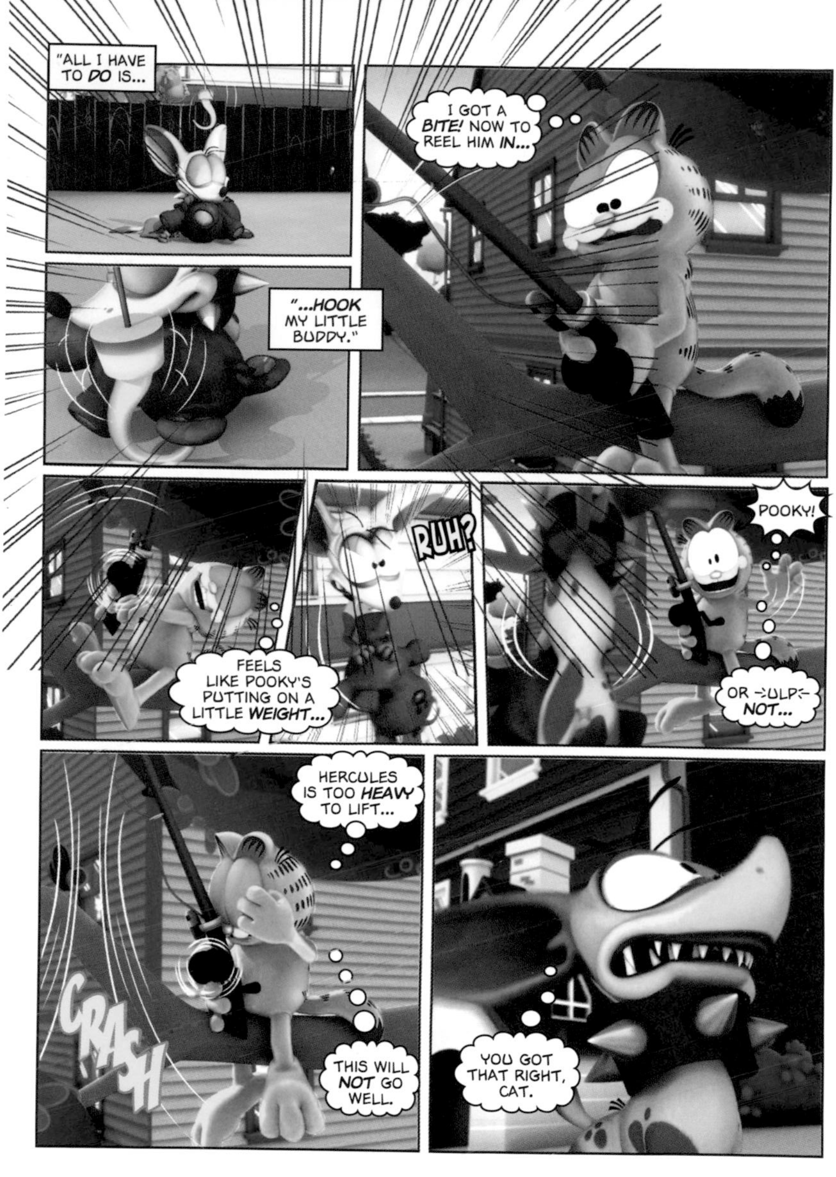

"ALL I HAVE TO DO IS...
I GOT A BITE! NOW TO REEL HIM IN...
"...HOOK MY LITTLE BUDDY."
FEELS LIKE POOKY'S PUTTING ON A LITTLE WEIGHT...
RUH?
POOKY!
OR -ULP- NOT...
HERCULES IS TOO HEAVY TO LIFT...
CRASH
THIS WILL NOT GO WELL.
YOU GOT THAT RIGHT, CAT.

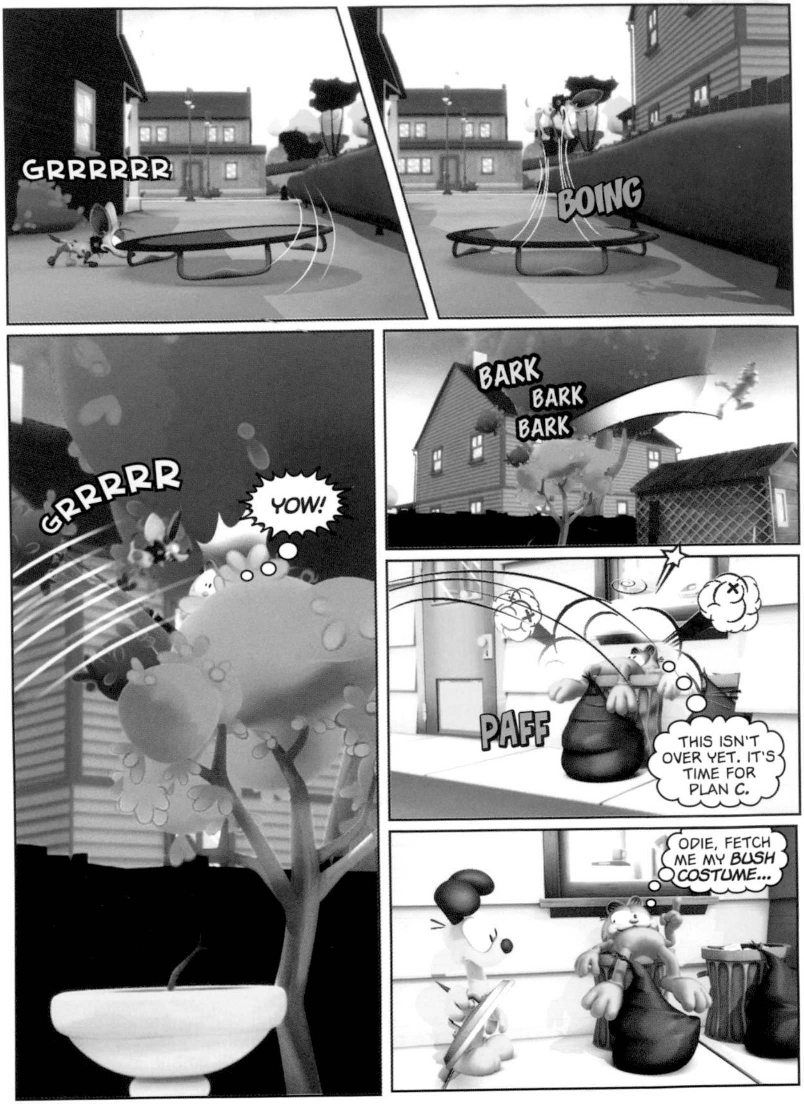
GRRRRRR
BOING
GRRRRR
YOW!
BARK
BARK
BARK
PAFF
THIS ISN'T OVER YET. IT'S TIME FOR PLAN C.
ODIE, FETCH ME MY BUSH COSTUME...

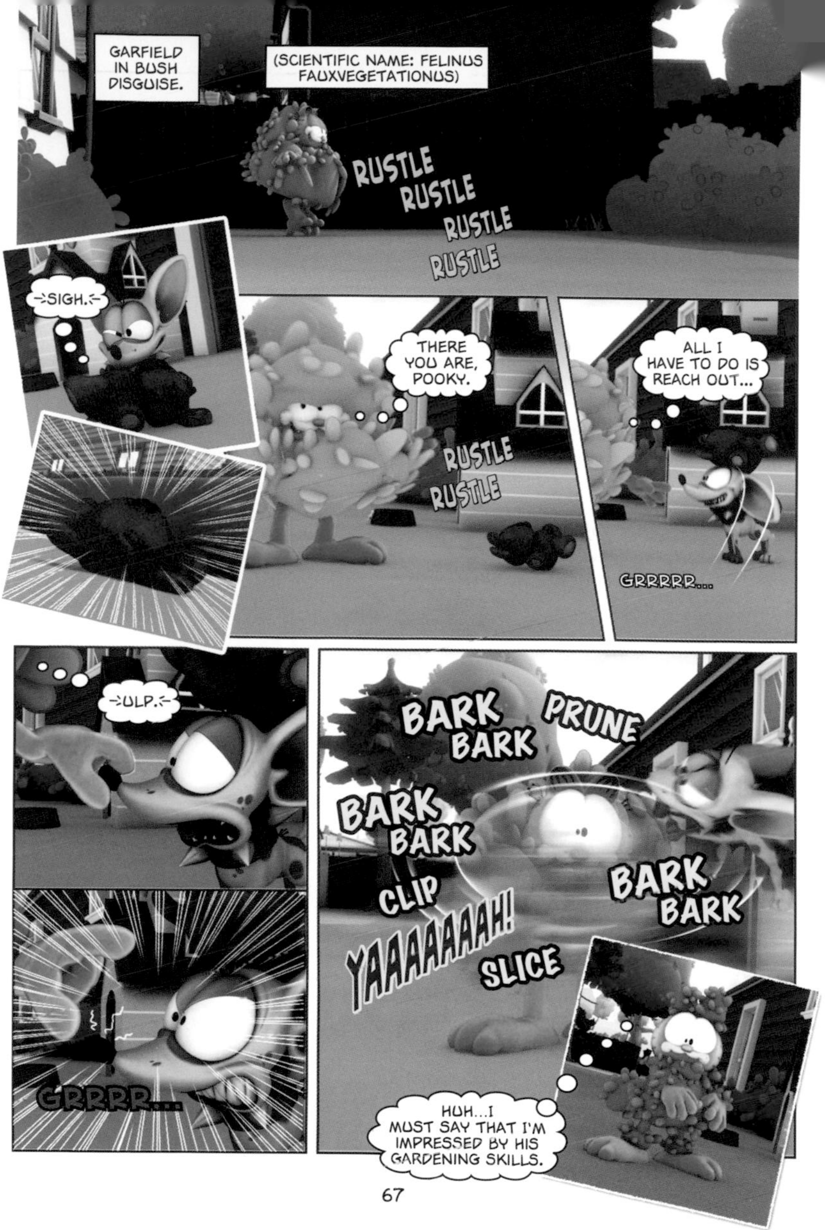

GARFIELD IN BUSH DISGUISE.
(SCIENTIFIC NAME: FELINUS FAUXVEGETATIONUS)
RUSTLE
RUSTLE
RUSTLE
RUSTLE
SIGH.
THERE YOU ARE, POOKY.
RUSTLE
RUSTLE
ALL I HAVE TO DO IS REACH OUT...
GRRRRR...
ULP.
GRRRR...
BARK
BARK
PRUNE
BARK
BARK
CLIP
BARK
BARK
YAAAAAAH!
SLICE
HUH...I MUST SAY THAT I'M IMPRESSED BY HIS GARDENING SKILLS.

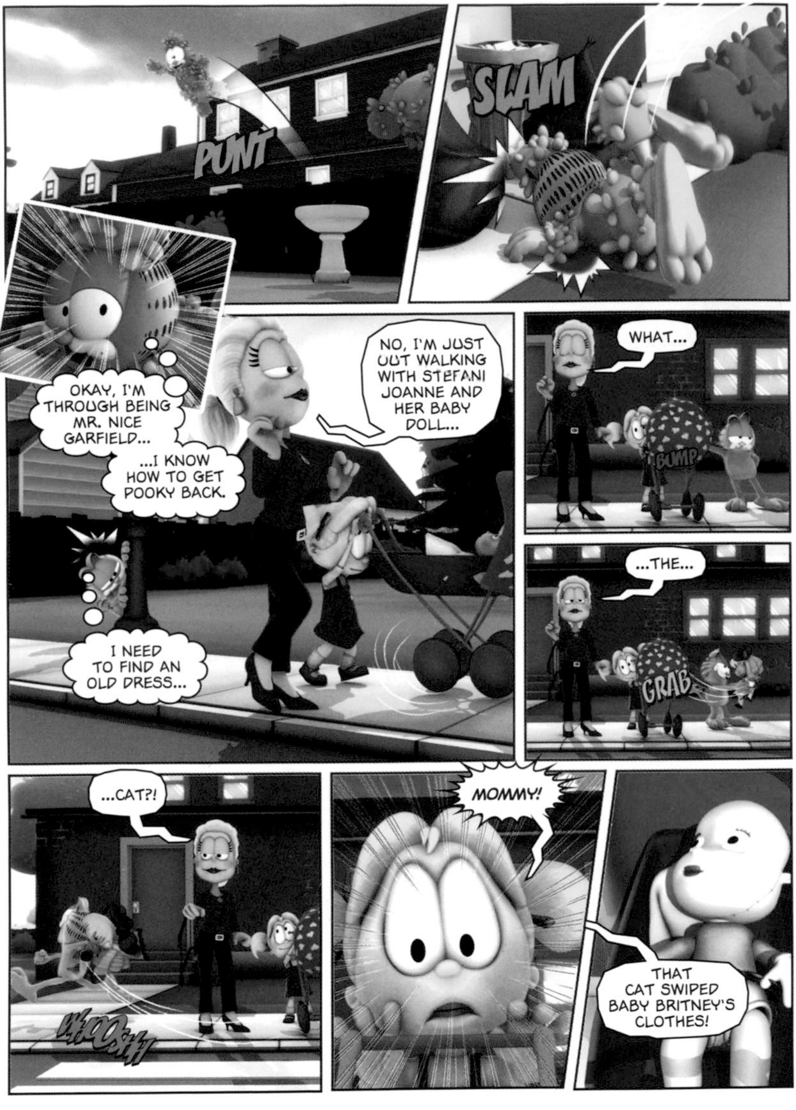
PUNT
SLAM
OKAY, I'M THROUGH BEING MR. NICE GARFIELD...
...I KNOW HOW TO GET POOKY BACK.
I NEED TO FIND AN OLD DRESS...
NO, I'M JUST OUT WALKING WITH STEFANI JOANNE AND HER BABY DOLL...
WHAT...
BUMP
...THE...
GRAB
...CAT?!
WHOOSHH
MOMMY!
THAT CAT SWIPED BABY BRITNEY'S CLOTHES!

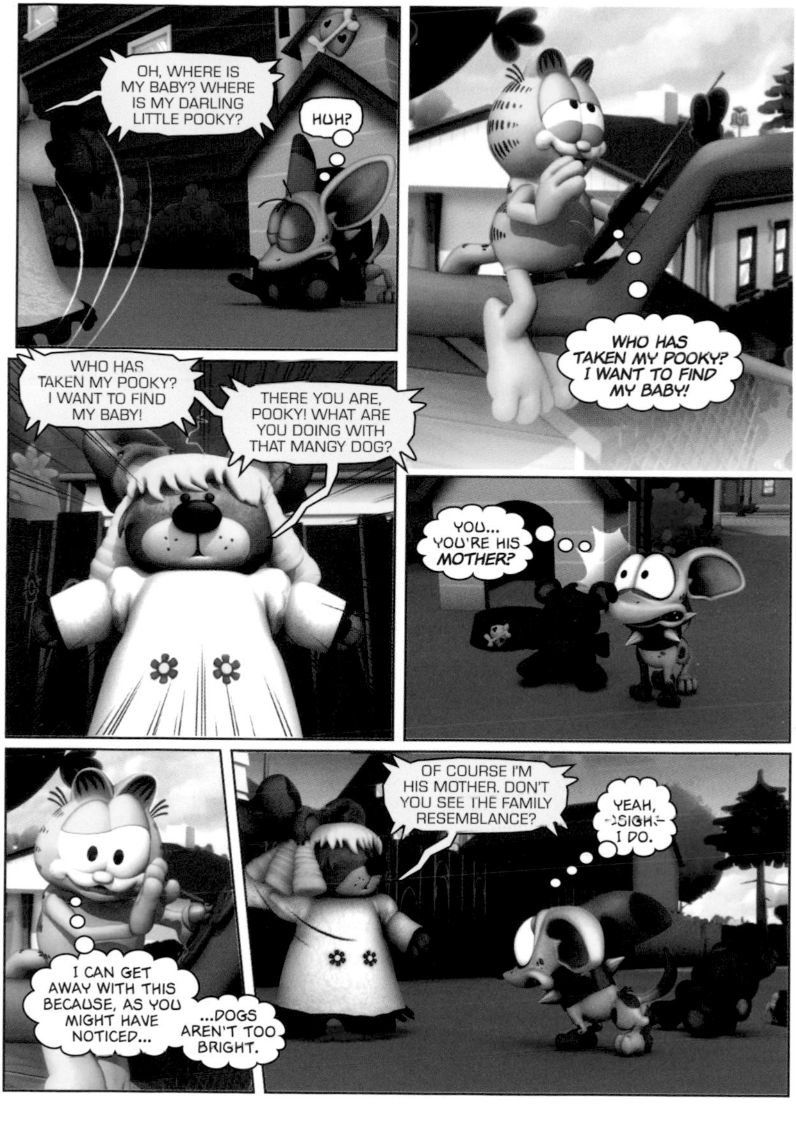
OH, WHERE IS MY BABY? WHERE IS MY DARLING LITTLE POOKY?
HUH?
WHO HAS TAKEN MY POOKY? I WANT TO FIND MY BABY!
WHO HAS TAKEN MY POOKY? I WANT TO FIND MY BABY!
THERE YOU ARE, POOKY! WHAT ARE YOU DOING WITH THAT MANGY DOG?
YOU... YOU'RE HIS MOTHER?
I CAN GET AWAY WITH THIS BECAUSE, AS YOU MIGHT HAVE NOTICED...
...DOGS AREN'T TOO BRIGHT.
OF COURSE I'M HIS MOTHER. DON'T YOU SEE THE FAMILY RESEMBLANCE?
YEAH, -SIGH- I DO.

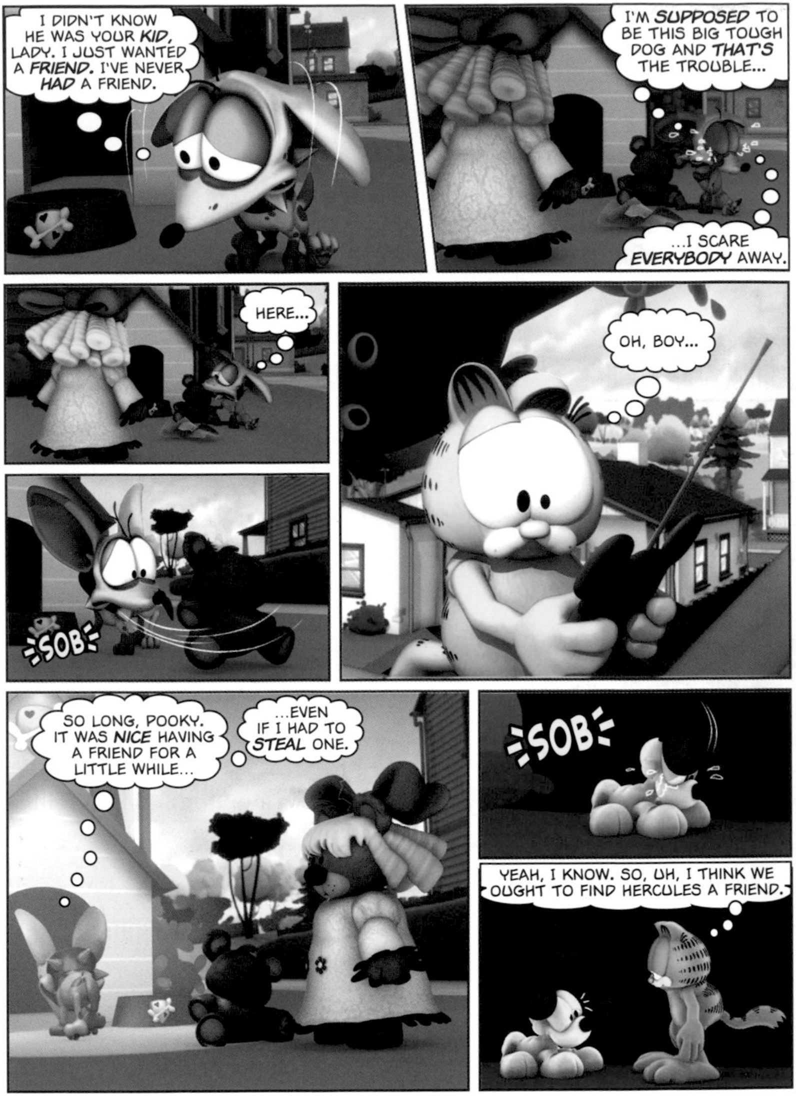
I DIDN'T KNOW HE WAS YOUR KID, LADY. I JUST WANTED A FRIEND. I'VE NEVER HAD A FRIEND.
I'M SUPPOSED TO BE THIS BIG TOUGH DOG AND THAT'S THE TROUBLE...
...I SCARE EVERYBODY AWAY.
HERE...
OH, BOY...
SOB
SO LONG, POOKY. IT WAS NICE HAVING A FRIEND FOR A LITTLE WHILE...
...EVEN IF I HAD TO STEAL ONE.
SOB
YEAH, I KNOW. SO, UH, I THINK WE OUGHT TO FIND HERCULES A FRIEND.

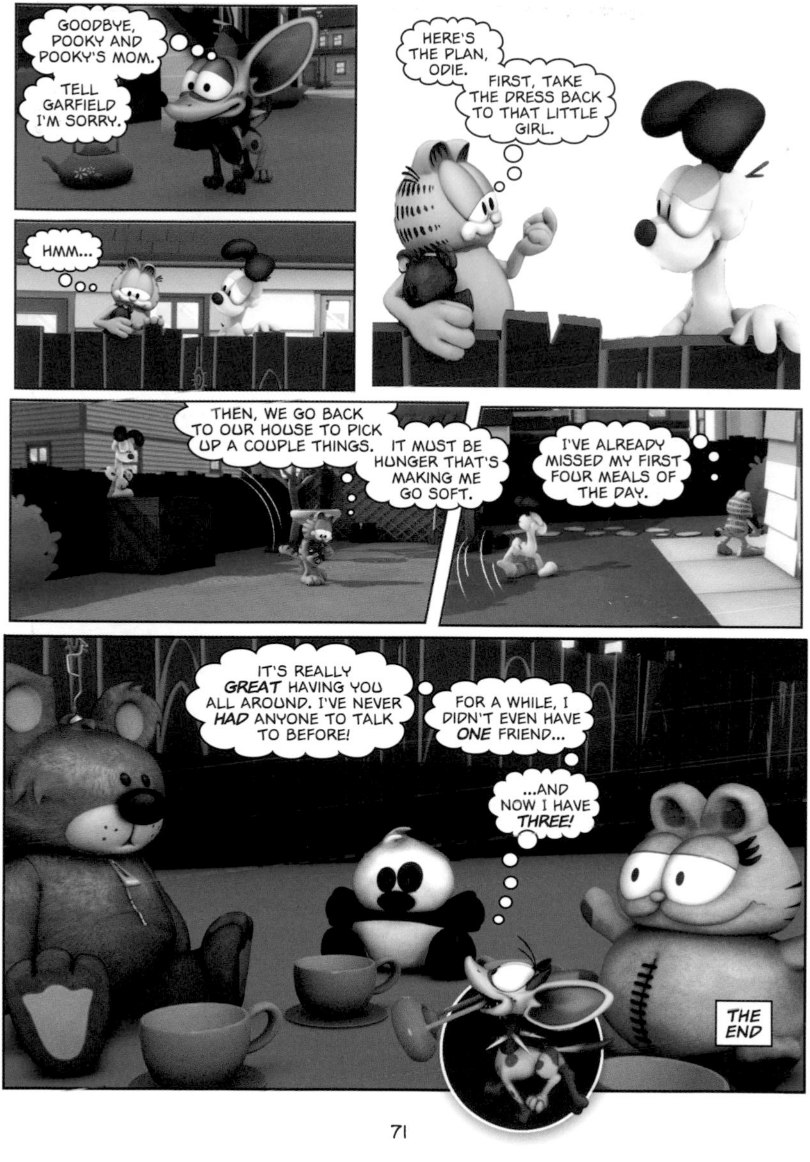
GOODBYE, POOKY AND POOKY'S MOM.
TELL GARFIELD I'M SORRY.
HMM...
HERE'S THE PLAN, ODIE.
FIRST, TAKE THE DRESS BACK TO THAT LITTLE GIRL.
THEN, WE GO BACK TO OUR HOUSE TO PICK UP A COUPLE THINGS.
IT MUST BE HUNGER THAT'S MAKING ME GO SOFT.
I'VE ALREADY MISSED MY FIRST FOUR MEALS OF THE DAY.
IT'S REALLY GREAT HAVING YOU ALL AROUND. I'VE NEVER HAD ANYONE TO TALK TO BEFORE!
FOR A WHILE, I DIDN'T EVEN HAVE ONE FRIEND...
...AND NOW I HAVE THREE!
THE END

WATCH OUT FOR PAPERCUTZ™

Welcome to the somewhat-smaller, scale-tipping, stuffed-animal-seeking, self-swapping, seventh THE GARFIELD SHOW graphic novel, based on the original characters created by Jim Davis, from Papercutz, those deficient dieticians devoted to publishing great graphic novels for all ages. I'm Jim Salicrup, Editor-in-Chief and fellow lasagna-lover, here to offer up some exciting news...

The most obvious—we've added more pages... again! For those of you who remember when Papercutz first published GARFIELD & Co #1 "Fish to Fry" back in 2011, you'll recall that graphic novel was a slim 32 pages. After an additional seven GARFIELD & Co graphic novels, we then launched the current THE GARFIELD SHOW series, which up until now, has been a pleasingly plump 64 pages each. Now, starting with this seventh volume, THE GARFIELD SHOW graphic novels have increased in size to a whopping 72 pages! Like Garfield himself, his graphic novels just keep getting fatter and fatter!

But the increase in page count isn't all that has changed. The height and width of THE GARFIELD SHOW graphic novels has been reduced. We're now a littler bigger book. The reason is slightly complicated, but if you're curious to find out the answer, I'm here to give it to you. But first a very short history lesson...

The animated *Garfield* TV series has been produced in France and seen all over the world. Originally, a French comics (*bande dessinée* or *BD* as it's called there) publisher was reformating the artwork created for the TV series to create the graphic novels (or "graphic albums" as they're called in Europe). The French publisher edited the stories to appeal to a very, very young audience, and even greatly abridged some stories, to be able to squeeze three GARFIELD stories into each of their graphic novels. We at Papercutz were attempting to restore as much of the original dialogue from the TV episodes as possible, and to maintain the style of the original GARFIELD comic strips for our audience..

Recently, a comics publisher in China started adapting the animated GARFIELD shows, also repurposing the animated artwork, and more importantly, they're not drastically abridging the stories. Each story is being adapted into 23 full pages of comics, as opposed to just 12 or (⇒Gasp!⇐) 5 pages, which has been the case up until now. Given the opportunity to switch to that material, we grabbed it! The only catch is that the standard Chinese comics format is a little smaller in height and width than what we were publishing up until now, but we thought the greater fidelity to the source material made it worth it. We hope you agree.

Ant that's the long and short of it! Don't miss THE GARFIELD SHOW #8, coming soon, for three more adventures of everyone's favorite orange fat cat!

Thanks,

Jim

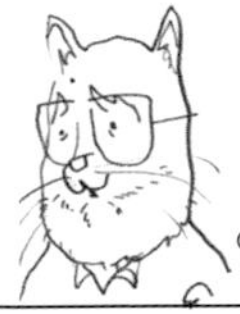

CARICATURE OF JIM BY ORTHO

STAY IN TOUCH!

EMAIL:	SALICRUP@PAPERCUTZ.COM
WEB:	PAPERCUTZ.COM
TWITTER:	@PAPERCUTZGN
INSTAGRAM:	@PAPERCUTZGN
FACEBOOK:	PAPERCUTZGRAPHICNOVELS
U.S.P.S.:	PAPERCUTZ, 160 BROADWAY, SUITE 700, EAST WING, NEW YORK, NY 10038